FROM TEENAGE RUNAWAY TO CLASS PRESIDENT

BOY
AT THE
CROSSROADS

A NOVEL INSPIRED BY A TRUE STORY

MARY FORD

The author has tried to recreate events, locales, and conversations from her husband's memories of them. In order to maintain their anonymity, in some instances, she has changed the names of individuals. Many parts of his story have been fictionalized in varying degrees, including dialogue.

FOR SAMANTHA

Publishing Services provided by Paper Raven Books

Printed in the United States of America

First Printing, 2021

Paperback ISBN= 978-1-7363164-0-5
Hardback ISBN= 978-1-7363164-1-2

PROLOGUE

Dedicated to: Lee J. and Cora Ford and their sixteen children: Ray, Edith, Ethel, Pauline, Betty, Henry, Bill, Mary, Nona, Don, Dana, Joe, David, Annie, Conley, and Junior.

Three questions rattled around in my head for years. How was I able to run off at thirteen and live on my own? How did I become self-reliant at such a young age? Why was I more at home, away from home?

There are no simple answers.

For one thing, my family was enormous. My mother gave birth to sixteen children. I was number fifteen.

Our pride kept us from thinking we were poor. Dad, who worked us hard, accepted no charity and often gave our food or clothing away if someone needed it more than we did.

Dad was home on Sundays, his day off from the railroad, and therefore, a work day for us. One of his favorite sayings was *if God said Sunday was a day of rest— he didn't say all day long.*

If we Fords weren't digging a well, peddling Mom's hot tamales door-to-door, or doing a shitload of chores— we were either at school or old enough to hold a paying job.

There was no affection in our house, no hugs, no kisses. No warmth, no tenderness. Being loved was understood. No one ever expressed it outwardly. Love meant being fed, clothed, and having a place to sleep. It was years before I realized other families were different.

I was an adult before I understood why Mom and Dad were like that. By the time I arrived in 1942, they were in their early forties and seemed old. Some of my pals had grandparents that age.

Born in southeastern Kentucky at the turn of the twentieth century, my parents each had one foot firmly planted in the nineteenth. They came from poor, old-time families which didn't put a lot of stock in coddling their children.

Mom was a Hall—a Harlan County, Kentucky family noted for being the gentler folks in a lawless place. In the

1920s when Cora was a young married woman, Harlan County had more murders than anywhere in the country.

The Hall men were kindhearted but had a weakness for whiskey. After a night of drinking, my grandfather Joseph Emmitt Hall was left by the roadside to die after being struck by a car. My uncle Walton grew skinny from alcoholism. His shock of white hair was in sharp contrast to a pair of eyes so blue you could see into his soul. Walton told me how he loved shoveling coal.

"The temperature in the mines is the same all year round," he recalled. "Like a warm kitchen in winter and like a cool breeze in summertime."

The work was steady, and the life of a coal miner was all Walton knew and all his brothers and their father had known before him. The fourteen Hall children—seven of whom died young—grew up in a coal company camp on Black Mountain.

My father, Lee J. Ford, had a booming voice when he wanted to make a point, which he did, often. He wasn't fair and blue-eyed like Mom but dark-haired, dark-eyed, and short-fused with none of the patience mother was blessed with.

Dad—a big, striking man and lifelong teetotaler with a fondness for foul language and tall tales—had a mean streak.

Folks always said that "was the Ford in him." Dad's father, Isom, was even meaner, and his brother, my uncle Wiley Ford, was so mean that his wife tried to kill Wiley with some poisonous berries mixed in with blackberry cobbler. Her plan backfired. Afterwards, Wiley—who got sick with stomach pains—kept a loaded revolver by his dinner plate. That kept Laura, the mother of their six children, in fear for her life, prompting her to ask her brothers for help.

Her brothers lay in wait one evening under the front porch. They shot the tall, lanky Wiley right through the forehead as he ducked down under the garden arbor to walk up the front path.

As years passed, "the Ford in her or him" became the justification for unusual behaviors and conditions in my family. When at just fourteen, my sister Pauline ran off to Detroit into the arms of an older man—it was the Ford in her. When my brother Don hit Dad over the head with the meat tenderizer mallet, that was the Ford in him too.

Even when my brother Bill got sick with a mental disorder—it was whispered that being a Ford was at the root of his breakdown.

Dad was the youngest of seven and so sickly that Isom and my grandmother—who had lost two children by the time he was born—didn't bother to name him until he was around four years old. As my Dad told it, a preacher stopped by and asked them, "what is that one called?" and getting no response, gave him a name.

For the place and times, Dad was an educated man. Too young to go to war in 1917 and being a skinny, weakling of a teenager, seemingly ill-equipped for hard labor, Dad showed an interest in school. He attended Tinsley School in Trosper and Union College in Barbourville. In May of 1918, at just seventeen, he was awarded a certificate to teach in the common schools of Knox County, Kentucky.

But the opportunity to become a teletype operator for the L&N Railroad, which was looking for men who could read and write, ended any future teaching career for Dad.

By twenty, my father had filled out and was described as handsome. He and the pretty, blue-eyed Cora got married and were known as the best-looking couple in Harlan County.

Mom and Dad with their seven children left Harlan County when Wiley's killers, after just five years in the state penitentiary, were paroled. Dad had lived with Wiley and his family when he started working for the railroad. He testified against the brothers at the murder trial, and word traveled fast they'd settle the score.

In fear for their lives, Dad collected Mom and the children in the middle of the night and moved through the Cumberland Gap to Knoxville, Tennessee.

Mom's formal education went no further than the eighth grade, but what she lacked in book learning she made up for in resourcefulness. She made her own clothes and the girls' dresses; she could crochet, embroider and quilt.

Proud of her Kentucky roots, Mom often said: *You cannot trust people from Tennessee,* even though she grew up less than a hundred miles away on the other side of the mountains. Another of her favorite sayings was: *Beware of a man who comes to the door with his sleeves rolled up.*

Mom also believed you could tell a baby boy's fortune by putting a deck of cards, a Bible, and a bottle of whiskey on the floor. Whichever item the baby crawled to would be the life they would live: becoming a gambler, alcoholic, or preacher.

Alcohol played a continuing role in her family. When Mom's eldest sister died, our cousin Bob—who was a preacher and chief of police—locked up uncles Walton and Ken in the Evarts jailhouse overnight. He wanted to be sure they'd be sober for their sister's funeral.

As the years passed, Mom was relieved that none of her sons had turned to whiskey as her father and brothers had. And Dad, who witnessed the evils of liquor in Harlan, didn't allow any alcohol in the house.

The Ford kids came in thirds. The oldest third I only knew as adults because they'd left home for the most part. The middle third, I looked up to a lot. They were in their teens when I was very young. The bottom third consisting of Joe, David, Annie, and me grew up together.

Being at the tail end of a herd of children meant I was always trying to get a seat at the big table at mealtime and to reach for more than a chicken neck or wing as the dinner platter was passed.

Annie, who was sixteen months older than me, and I sat at a small table beside the circular oak dining table because there was not enough room for us. We looked forward to moving to the Big Table, with Annie certain she would go up first, being older. But as it turned out, two of our siblings moved out at the same time, opening up two spots. This is when we learned that there was more to chicken than necks and wings.

With so many of us—and the Fords were known for strong personalities—eating together was often coupled with arguments, prompting Mom to call for quiet. If we didn't listen, Dad would stand up and say, "God damn it—your mother told you to shut up!" Then he would yank the tablecloth, spilling the dinner plates all over our laps and the floor and demand the girls clean it up.

On those evenings, I went to bed hungry with a nervous stomach. Hugging my legs, I curled up in a tight ball, and thought about how much I loathed my Dad, and dreamt about taking off as soon as I could.

Chapter One

JOYRIDING

M y brief stint as a car thief started after my family moved to Dry Gap Pike near Halls Crossroads. I hankered to see friends in the old neighborhood in North Knoxville where I'd spent twelve years. On Saturdays when I could get away, I hitched to my sister Betty's. Her family had moved into our old house on East Scott Avenue, which gave me a destination. It was on one of those trips that I met Wyatt.

Wyatt E. Mountain was cool: for one thing, he had his driver's license. He spoke like he knew what he was talking about; carried an entire pack of Lucky Strikes twisted in the short sleeve of his t-shirt; and had a couple of cousins who lived near me in Halls.

When I was a city boy, I either hoofed it or hopped on a bus so I was a latecomer to hitchhiking. But I made up for lost time after moving to the country when thumbing became my chief mode of transportation.

But no amount of hitching could compare to cruising around in a car with my buddies, even if the ride didn't exactly belong to us.

For that reason, Wyatt didn't have a tough time persuading me to go along on his escapades in stolen Mercury sedans.

Tall and skinny with a slicked black pompadour, Wyatt had stubble on his chin and upper lip that made him look tough.

The day I met Wyatt, he was visiting his buddy Paul, whose grandmother moved in across the street from Betty's. I introduced myself and easily struck up a conversation with the two boys about our schools and where we grew up.

"I'm Conley Ford and my big sis Betty lives over there." I pointed to the big white house. "That was my house before my Dad up and moved us last year. We lived on East Scott for ages, and I know just about everybody on the street."

The guys seemed impressed when I rattled off the names of the families in each house and most of the residents in the Peters Apartments. Holding their attention made me feel like somebody.

After about half an hour of chitchat, Paul's grandmother called him to finish chores and Wyatt glanced toward me.

"Hey you, I'm heading to St. Mary's to find something to drive. Wanna come?"

I wasn't entirely clear on what Wyatt meant by "something to drive"—but always being up for an adventure, was curious to find out.

"Me?" I looked around stupidly as I pointed at my chest. Of course, it was me, I thought. I was the only one standing there.

"Yeah, you."

Wyatt motioned to me to tag along on the ten-minute walk to the hospital on East Oak Hill Avenue.

Wyatt walked fast and didn't have much small talk. Like a guy with important places to go, he glanced at his nifty Timex wristwatch with brown leather band. He was the first boy I knew that had a watch. The rest of us had to guess the time of day but were never far off. We rose with the sun and let growls in our bellies dictate when it was time to eat. It was bedtime when we couldn't keep our eyes open.

Wyatt had a cigarette going most of the time that he lit with a Zippo lighter with a silver quarter glued to the front. Tossing a cigarette into his mouth with his left hand, Wyatt popped the top of the Zippo and struck the flint wheel with his right thumb in a continuous motion.

"Why'd you stick a quarter on the lighter?" I got up the nerve to ask.

Wyatt stopped and showed me the quarter close-up. The date on it was 1939.

"That's the year I was born," he said.

My eyes lit up and I knew right then, the first chance I got, I'd get myself a Zippo and glue a 1942 quarter to it.

Once at St. Mary's, we spent about an hour in the parking lot watching people get in and out of their cars. Being able to spot a car's year, make, and model, along with the details that made each of them different, were part of our vocabulary.

Sitting under the branches of a magnolia tree on a slight rise at the edge of the parking lot, we kicked up the bright reddish dirt with our feet. To pass the time Wyatt made smoke rings that rose like bubbles while I chewed on a long strand of dried crab grass.

Wyatt stayed focused on any Mercurys. At first that surprised me because they were not the snazziest of cars. If I was picking—the Pontiac Chieftan, Catalina Coupe, and the Buick Roadmaster Skylark were far superior.

"Want a piece of gum?" Wyatt offered, extending a pack of Juicy Fruit with a stick of gum poking out. I nodded and grabbed the gum. As I wadded up the foil wrapper, Wyatt stopped me from tossing it.

"Hey, I need that."

I shrugged and handed him the foil.

"That's my key," he said.

I'll admit to being a little intimidated by Wyatt and didn't want to seem like a birdbrain. It took me a while to muster the courage to ask how he'd start a car using a gum wrapper.

Like a big brother, Wyatt explained how he looked for unlocked 1952 and 1953 Mercurys with gas in the tank. His fingernails were stained with grease, a sure sign he knew his way around an engine. Using his hands to demonstrate, he showed me how those Mercury models had an open space under the dashboard where three wires terminate behind the ignition switch. A small piece of tinfoil pushed up in there triggered the starter.

We spotted only two Mercurys, which were both locked and had been parked for a while. Wyatt said it was time to give up looking, and we headed back.

On the way to Scott Avenue we wandered along a street behind Sears and Wyatt finally offered me a smoke from his deck of Luckies. As he was giving me a light, he eyed a handsome, brand-new Chevy Bel Air parked at the curb with spiffy clipper hubcaps.

"I'll sell these fast and make a few bucks." Wyatt gave the driver's side wheel a couple of quick kicks and crouched down. "Keep a look out."

Not fancying getting into trouble with the law in my old neighborhood, I fidgeted at the corner about ten cars away while Wyatt tried to swipe the hubcaps. There were locks on the valve stems so we abandoned the plan and got back to Paul's grandmother's house.

With a flat top, no sideburns, and a round face, Paul wasn't as cool as Wyatt. But they'd come up through grade school together and shared some history. Wyatt tossed Paul a cigarette and then gave him a light with his Zippo. He didn't toss me one.

About to enjoy their smokes, the two buddies leaned against the trunk of the 1948 Plymouth belonging to Paul's grandmother. I took it as a hint it was time for me to go.

I spent that night at Betty's. My brother-in-law Glen gave me a ride back to Dry Gap Pike the next morning.

A week later when I was back at Betty's, Wyatt showed up in a shiny, admiral blue 1952 Mercury, two-door sedan with whitewall tires that were totally boss. Paul was at his grandmother's and had some free time so we hopped in the car. There were no keys in the ignition and the chariot had a full tank.

I had the back seat to myself and admired the twin ashtrays as I lit a smoke. The light gray cloth seat was spotless so I was careful not to drop an ash. As we drove, Wyatt and Paul positioned the front vent windows just right so the wind hit my face.

As we toured up and down the hills in neighborhoods all over Knoxville, I looked right and left as we sped by houses and city buildings. I didn't want the afternoon to end. Wyatt turned up the radio loud when the new chart-topper "Maybellene" by Chuck Berry came on and the three of us joined in the refrain at the top of our voices.

Late that afternoon, Wyatt gave me a ride home to Dry Gap Pike. It was the first time I'd ever gone for a joyride and I loved it.

As I got busy with farm work, the start of school, and new friends, I didn't see Wyatt and Paul again for weeks.

But just a few days before I started the eighth grade, a pale gray Mercury sedan pulled up our driveway on a hot, late August afternoon.

Wyatt said he'd taken the car from St. Mary's Hospital. My best buddy Roger from the old neighborhood waved to me from the back seat. On the smaller side, Roger looked a little lost back there.

"Hey, Conley. What's buzzin', cuzzin'?"

"Hey, Rog. What's up?"

We gave each other a thumbs-up.

As it turned out, Roger met Wyatt at Paul's grandmother's when he was on his paper route.

Wyatt told me to get in and I couldn't think of a reason not to. Dad wasn't home that afternoon and no one but me had seen them drive up.

Tickled to be asked to go, I jumped into the sedan and for a couple of hours, the four of us hauled ass on unpaved, back roads all over the county. Wyatt liked spinning the wheels on dirt roads by flooring the gas pedal and watching the needle on the fuel gauge go down.

We flew over roller-coaster roads as "Rock Around the Clock" with Bill Haley and the Comets blared on the radio. The Merc had manual transmission so Wyatt could shift down around sharp curves without burning rubber. Roger and I held onto the back of the front seat to keep from falling over.

With no money and a near-empty tank, Wyatt talked about selling the spare tire if he could pry the trunk open. But not wanting to get stranded, he dropped me off at the foot of my long, gravel driveway before looking for another Mercury.

Still flying high, I couldn't stop smiling as I trekked up the steep hill. I swear my feet barely touched the ground as I kept pace with the "Rock Around the Clock" lyrics running through my head.

It was a Saturday afternoon about three weeks later when I finished my chores and decided to hitch back to Betty's.

Wyatt, who'd picked Roger up, arrived at Paul's in a cool yellow Mercury ragtop. The car was like a magnet and I went right over.

Dark clouds threatened so we put the top up and the four of us took off driving around Knoxville then out Cumberland Avenue by the University of Tennessee heading toward Dixie Lee Junction.

In my mind, nothing could beat cruising around in a big car with the windows down and the radio blasting. The only thing that could top it would be getting my license and having my own wheels. We used our fingers to whistle at girls we passed and got a kick out of the astonished looks they gave us.

As we headed toward Lenoir City in Loudon County and with a near empty gas tank, Wyatt starting looking for another Mercury.

"You guys keep your eyes peeled," he said.

In Lenoir City, we spotted a black 1952 Mercury parked on a quiet street; we inched by slowly to check it out. Wyatt and Paul then let Roger and me off about a block away and drove to the unlocked car that had about half a tank of gas. As a light rain started to fall, they ditched the first car, then picked us up in the second car, and we took off. I was so cranked I rattled off a bunch of words in rapid succession like "this is crazy!" prompting Wyatt to tell me to cool it.

Around 10 p.m., we came upon a rural country store in a fork in the road where Wyatt said we needed supplies.

I sat in the driver's seat with my hands gripping the wheel in the running car with the lights out, as the other boys pried open a window. Roger was small enough to be lifted through the opening. Once inside, he passed cartons of cigarettes and a load of candy to Wyatt and Paul, who burst out laughing at the haul. Roger helped himself to handfuls of pennies, the only money in the cash register, and put them in his pants pockets.

We couldn't open the trunk so they flung the stuff into the passenger seat. I climbed over the driver's seat into the back seat with Roger and we sped away. Roger, who was sandy-haired and fair, always turned bright red when excited. He looked redder than I'd ever seen him.

"Wow, that was something'," Wyatt yelped, as he floored it.

Paul tossed Roger and me each a candy bar. Starving, I ripped off the wrapper and devoured the Butterfinger that melted in my mouth. Candy was a treat under any circumstances and the stolen Butterfinger was super tasty. I licked any traces of chocolate off the empty wrapper.

"Yum! That was crazy good," I said, hoping for seconds. But Paul only smiled and nodded; sadly, no more candy flew into the back seat.

At just twelve and thirteen years old, Roger and I went along with whatever Wyatt said, including his decision to bury some of our loot. I got what we were doing was wrong, but that didn't stop me. I was too engulfed in the thrill of the moment.

The rain turned to drizzle as we traveled up a muddy road; we pulled over to the shoulder and left the car idling. In a nearby wooded area covered with wet leaves, we furiously dug a hole with our bare hands and buried the lion's share of the candy and cigarettes. We kept what we were going to eat and smoke that night.

When we got into the car to leave, Wyatt then hit the gas pedal too hard, spinning the wheels and causing the car to slip sideways into a ditch.

"What the hell happened?" Wyatt yelled. Paul, Roger and I climbed out, got behind the car, and tried to push it out of the mud.

"Shit! Get something to put underneath the rear tires," Wyatt said.

Working together, we uprooted a post from an old three-strand, barbed-wire fence and put it under the rear wheels to gain traction. We cheered as we got the car going again. I was happy despite having to suck out a toothpick-sized splinter from by right palm that hurt like hell.

Lulled into silence by the hum of the V-8 engine, we drove around for a while looking for a place to pull over and get some sleep. After we found a spot on a dirt road just past a church, the blur of approaching car lights got our attention. Through the darkness and slight drizzle, we could barely make out that the lights were from a sheriff's car. Wyatt, who wasn't willing to take a chance we were mistaken, said we had to leave the car and escape through the woods.

"More than likely that's the sheriff," Wyatt said. "Let's get outta here!"

As the car pulled up behind the Mercury, we grabbed any smokes and candy we could stuff into our shirts and pants and took off on foot. We hightailed it in the pitch-black night dodging trees and ran like hound dogs chasing a fox through briars and high weeds.

My heart pounded, as I felt my way up and down the hills, slipping, falling, and getting covered with dirt. The whole way, the pennies in Roger's bulging pockets kept jingling. It was kind of comical. The noise helped keep my mind off the brutal briars that cut through our hands and forearms and snagged our pants.

It must have been around 11 p.m. when we reached a clearing and could see the silhouette of a barn in the moonlight. We ran as fast as we could toward the barn, only disturbing two cows, and climbed the ladder into the hayloft to spend the night. Drenched in our sweat and the rain, we buried ourselves in the warm hay.

I wasn't worried because my parents, believing I was at Betty's, wouldn't question why I didn't come home.

The night for me was strangely familiar. My new home on Dry Gap Pike—a winding, hilly road, mostly dotted with small farms and few houses—was about eight miles from North Knoxville, but it might as well have been a million.

When night fell on East Scott Avenue where I'd spent all my early years, I saw streetlights and heard noises from the constant traffic, train whistles, and hissing of buses. On cold, dreary days, a thick fog filled the outside air from coal soot as furnaces spewed smoke out the flues.

The dark sky at Dry Gap Pike was lit only by the stars and moon and the air was always clear. When I drifted off, I could hear the rustle of the wind in the trees, crickets chirping, and cows mooing. In the barn that night, those same sounds lulled me to sleep.

⸎⸎⸎⸎⸎⸎⸎⸎⸎⸎⸎⸎⸎⸎⸎⸎⸎⸎⸎⸎⸎⸎⸎

At daylight Wyatt thought it best to get out before the farmer caught us. We brushed stalk bits off our clothes and hair, climbed down from the loft, and ran as fast as we could out of the barn, across the pasture, and shrieked as we jumped a fence. We finally reached a paved road. From there it took us about thirty minutes to get back to the highway where we planned to hitch a ride to Knoxville. But, being early Sunday morning when most folks were in church, the two-lane road was deserted in both directions, apart from a family of red foxes crossing in the distance.

As time wore on, we got really hungry, having polished off the remaining candy we saved from the night before. As chance would have it, we spotted a small house set back off the road.

"I'm going to head up and investigate." Wyatt said he'd knock and if someone was home; he planned to tell them we were lost and looking for directions. Paul, Roger, and I followed along about twenty feet behind him.

No one answered, so Wyatt tried the door which opened easily. He signaled for us to come fast. We went inside and helped ourselves to freshly baked biscuits, which we slathered with homemade blackberry jam. Famished, we licked our fingers and made a mess of crumbs and jam on the kitchen table. Sticking our heads under the faucet, we gulped down some tap water. Roger grabbed a large box of Sun-Maid raisins off the counter before the four of us headed back to the highway.

This time despite our rumpled appearance, we were successful in getting a ride to Knoxville when an old Plymouth sedan stopped. Wyatt climbed in the front seat next to the driver and the rest of us got into the backseat. The car left us off on Cumberland Avenue close to the L&N Depot. As we started walking to East Scott Avenue, the rain picked up again so we ducked under a viaduct for about ten minutes to wait out the storm. We didn't say much. With a smile on my face, I was in high spirits and spent the time reflecting on our adventure.

Once on East Scott, I made my way back to Betty's house. Betty had no idea where I'd been. The looks of me likely signaled to her that I'd been engaging in high jinks.

"Connie, what happened to you?" she said.

My family had called me Connie since I was a baby. It was okay for them, but I didn't like it if other people did. It sounded like a girl's name.

"I spent the night with some friends." I hoped that was truthful enough.

Betty was my favorite sister and a second mother to me. She was the opposite of Mom. Betty's mouth was always painted with cherry-red lipstick that contrasted with her jet-black hair. She wore high heels and stylish dresses to her job as a switchboard operator at Southern Bell. Our Mom never wore makeup. She wore practical lace-up oxfords and her dresses were made of printed cotton feed sacks.

Betty understood me and bought me stuff from time to time like a super set of cat's eye marbles. When I was about seven, I had my eye on a kid's red bicycle in a small shop next to Cas Walker's grocery store. She spent a week's pay getting me that bike.

After Betty married, she quickly had two boys. She never gave up her job working nights as a switchboard operator. She loved it too much.

"Well, you look like you've been in the wars," she said. "Let me have those clothes."

Betty covered for me with Mom and Dad and said I'd spent the night at her house. She put my clothes in the wash, and that afternoon Glen took me home.

Glen was a man of few words, so I spent the ride thinking I'd gotten away with something. This joyriding gig was a gas.

Chapter Two

THE MERCURY GANG

On a late October morning, the principal sent a faculty member down to my homeroom to find me.

Detective Carl Bunch, a tall thin man in his thirties, and another officer were waiting in Principal Lakin's office. Both men wore dark business suits not police uniforms; they looked serious. To a thirteen-year-old, eighth-grader like me, they could've been FBI.

Unbeknownst to me, I was part of what the police had named the "Mercury Gang." They were looking for suspects in a rash of car thefts. The Mercury sedan, which broke the case for them, was the one my buddies and I abandoned that dark night in Loudon County when we saw the sheriff's car approaching.

"I'd like to talk to you, Conley," Bunch said as he sat on the edge of the principal's desk with one foot on the floor and his other foot dangling halfway down. He was wearing newly shined black leather shoes with laces, and the strap to his shoulder holster was peeking out from under his suit jacket.

"Have you been involved in stealing cars?"

With his arms folded and standing by the window, Mr. Lakin listened with a disapproving frown on his face but didn't say a word. I sat facing his desk in a chair that had housed many a student about to get a detention for playing hooky or cussing out a classmate—but likely never one accused of a real crime.

Figuring lying could make matters worse, I said, "Yes, sir," right off.

"Then you need to come with us, son."

I wasn't handcuffed as the two detectives walked me between them out of school. Hoping my schoolmates wouldn't notice, I kept my head down as we made our way to an unmarked police car.

I climbed into the backseat for the ten-mile drive from Halls Crossroads to the Knoxville Police Station.

"Geez, there are no door handles or window cranks back here," I mumbled as the detectives got in the front.

I wondered how many crooks sat here. "Am I gonna be locked up?" I wondered and swallowed hard.

It was a warm fall day and the leaves were turning orange, yellow, and red on the hillsides. I tried to silence my pounding heart by staring out the window at all the colors that seemed like a movie reel.

While I'd imagined riding in a police car would be the coolest—I was glad I wasn't in a black-and-white with emergency lights flashing.

Sensing my unease, Detective Bunch turned and offered me a cigarette poking out from a pack of Camels. I was too upset to accept it. Along the way, Detective Bunch asked questions about my experiences with the stolen Mercurys. My voice cracked a couple of times. I responded "Yes, sir" or "No, sir."

<hr />

As we drove along, I thought about the summer before last when Roger and me almost went to jail for stealing golf balls.

We'd been playing at the rock quarry at Sharp's Gap in North Knoxville. We couldn't believe our luck when we found a slew of golf balls as we explored the creek bed.

One by one, we filled our pockets with the golf balls from the shallow creek under the Clinton Highway bridge that led to a huge driving range. When our pockets bulged, we tucked in our shirts and stuffed more balls around our waists.

Just as we had our fill, I looked up to see a two-tone, black-and-white Buick Roadmaster convertible coming toward us. The Buick's wheels tore up the turf, sending green grass bits flying when it skidded to a stop.

Roger jumped back and slipped, spilling a few golf balls as his shirt came loose. My mouth dropped when I recognized the driver from TV. It was Archie Campbell of the Country Playhouse.

The mustached Mr. Campbell spoke with authority as he ordered us into his car.

"You boys are going to jail for stealing."

"We're sorry, Mr. Campbell," we cried in unison, as we stood by dumbfounded.

We couldn't empty our pockets and shirts of golf balls fast enough into the pail he held out the driver's side. He had us believing we were going to be locked up for sure.

As I climbed into the car, I peeked over the driver's seat and saw Mr. Campbell, who had on a straw fedora, white sport coat, and blue shirt with no tie, was wearing black-and-white wingtips.

"This guy is a snappy dresser and to top it off, he's rich," I thought.

"Why'd you boys think you could steal my golf balls?"

Roger always relied on me to do the talking and frankly, I was the best choice. From a young age, fast talking had always come easily and got me out of some scrapes. Mom often said I was born talking.

"Mr. Campbell, we didn't think we were stealing. We just saw golf balls here and there, and thought they'd been lost."

"Uh-huh," he said.

"We were actually thinking about seeing if anyone, you know, might've lost them. But we hadn't yet made our plan when you drove up."

"Uh-huh."

I acted fast because I wasn't sure where Mr. Campbell's thinking was headed. Adding to my frustration was Roger's chin. It was quivering and he looked like he was going to bawl any second. My protective instincts for my friend took over.

"Mr. Campbell, we didn't know they were your golf balls. If we did, we would've left them right where they were at. Please, don't send us to jail or tell our folks. We promise never to pick up a golf ball again, ever!"

I thought I saw a small smile at the corner of Mr. Campbell's mouth but couldn't be sure.

"You boys should never take anything—including golf balls—unless you know for sure they belong to no one."

On the short car ride, Mr. Campbell had a change of heart before stopping to let us out at the corner of N. Central and Scott Avenue.

"You boys get out now and I never want to see you again."

"You mean we're not going to jail?" Roger squeaked as I jabbed him in the ribs with my elbow to get him to shut up.

"Now skedaddle!"

∞∞∞∞∞∞∞∞∞∞∞∞∞∞∞∞∞∞∞∞∞∞∞∞∞∞

When we got to the police station, I was put in the interrogation room alone where I sat sweating for half an hour. To stretch my legs, I got up and walked around the small, square table three times before sitting down. I stared at my hands and stupidly mumbled the Cas Walker's radio jingle over and over while jiggling my left leg, a nervous habit that drove my teachers crazy: *Get that Blue Ban Coffee and You'll Want No More. Do Your Grocery Shopping at the Cas Walker Store.*

Detective Bunch hadn't asked me about the other things we did that night: the country store we broke into, our sleeping in a farmer's barn, or helping ourselves to breakfast at the farmhouse.

I repeated in my head not to say more than asked. I could easily get carried away. Many of us Ford kids took after Dad, who could hold peoples' attention for hours with tales about working on the railroad.

A jailer finally came in and took me up the elevator to the third floor, then down a long hallway to a cell. There were three or four cells on the floor and only one was occupied where a scruffy-looking older man, snoring loudly, was sleeping it off. I got a whiff of whiskey as we walked by. I was used to seeing police pick up drunks in Happy Holler and take them into custody for their safety.

My musty-smelling cell looked just like the ones in the movies with a narrow bed, toilet, and sink. I sat on the bunk and bounced up and down with my butt, waiting to hear if the springs responded with a series of squeaks. But I discovered the thin mattress sat on top of a flat board attached to the wall. Since I was starving, I was happy when the jailer brought me a glass of water and a tray of white beans and cornbread that I wolfed down. I wondered out loud what I'd gotten into as I laid down with my arms folded behind my head.

I'd been up early to slop the hogs before school so by now, I was pretty tired and drifted off for a while. I dreamt about Florida—a place I'd only seen in pictures and on billboards. Often, when I was alone, I would repeat saying Flori-*da* under my breath with emphasis on the *da*. I loved orange juice, a treat we never had at home. I'd only tasted it a few times at a friend's house.

I wasn't alone in admiring Florida. Often East Tennesseans returning from a Florida vacation would strap a twenty-five-pound sack of oranges between the front fender and grille so everyone could see where they'd been.

By mid-afternoon, I still hadn't seen or talked to anyone in my family. But it was likely that no one missed me yet. Most of my siblings —while always law abiding—had run off at one time or another. The Fords were used to an empty seat or two at the table.

I woke with a start and jumped up when the jailer returned. He took me downstairs and turned me over to a uniformed deputy from the Loudon County Sheriff's Department who transported me to the Loudon County Jail. There I was fingerprinted and put in a holding cell where I was happy to see Roger; we smiled and eyeballed one other. I mouthed, "What happened to Paul and Wyatt?" but Roger only shrugged. I figured they'd also been arrested.

After about an hour, I was driven to the Juvenile Home on Euclid Avenue back in Knoxville, a place that looked like a school. Still in my school clothes, I was about to spend a restless night on a stiff cot in a bunk room that smelled like bleach with a handful of other delinquent boys.

No one had come to fetch me. In a way, I was relieved that I might've been forgotten. I wasn't ready to take the medicine Dad would dish out.

I counted the tiles on the wall, making it to 110 before my eyes finally closed.

The next morning after a breakfast of flour biscuits and sawmill sausage gravy in the cafeteria, I had to attend a general studies class. I couldn't focus on a single thing the teacher said.

Around noontime, I was released into the custody of my eldest brother Ray, who was twenty years older than me and had a law practice.

During the ride home in Ray's brand-new Ford Fairlane, we didn't talk about my arrest. I figured he was saving up any further discourse for our arrival. Instead, we reminisced about life on East Scott Avenue in North Knoxville before the family moved to Halls Crossroads.

As we approached our small farmhouse, the driveway seemed longer than before. I took a deep breath as Ray parked and we went inside.

Ray had told Mom and Dad that I could be looking at a year or two in reform school. Mom dabbed her tearful eyes with a white lace hanky. My brother David piped up and called me a moron. Dad told him to shut up.

I stared at the floor and nervously shuffled my right foot back 'n' forth. It didn't help that my fingertips were still stained from the inkpad at the Loudon County Jail.

"You're in a fine mess, Connie," was all Dad said.

I would've preferred a whipping than silence from Dad. Not knowing what might come next was torture.

All the Ford kids had an agonizing relationship with our father, who ran things with an iron fist. He was unwavering, controlling, dictatorial, and often cruel. Lazy was a four-letter word in our house. We yearned for a pat on the back that never came.

Dad's two favorite sayings were: *When you prop your feet under my table—you do as I say* and *The door swings this way and that, so if you go, don't come back the first night.* Over the years, most of us took this to heart and headed out the door.

Dad told Ray to do all he could to keep me out of reform school. He was worried I'd be influenced by bad boys and would embark on a lifetime of lawbreaking. My limited experience overnight at the Juvenile Home convinced me that reform school was not something I'd like.

Ray didn't stay for dinner, leaving me to fend for myself. Mom had the big pot of pinto beans with chili powder ready on the stove. The smell of fresh biscuits made me relax a little.

Being the youngest, it was my job to pick out the small rocks mixed in with the beans we bought in five-pound bags. I was thorough. Dental checkups in my family were nonexistent. Wrecking a molar on a small rock meant considerable pain, possible tooth loss, and a punch in the gut by the sufferer.

Dinner was quiet apart from the sound of our spoons and forks hitting the side of our plates. Dad wasn't happy but he never was, so I wasn't sure how to read him.

After dinner, he announced that I would have to move the pile of cinderblocks by the shed about 100 feet and stack them behind the outhouse. To make matters worse, he ordered David to help.

David and I argued the whole time. It took us over an hour to complete the task.

"This is your fault," said David, who was three years older but I was a lot taller.

"Get a life, shrimp!"

Our insults flew back and forth.

The bickering didn't help matters. When we were done, Dad ordered us to move all the cinderblocks back.

Ray went right to work on my case, taking me with him to get character references from a variety of people including Earl Graves, who owned the general store by the school bus stop at the end of Cunningham Road.

"Earl, this is my brother Ray." Earl was leaning on the counter by the cash register with the familiar #2 pencil perched on his right ear. "Ray has a favor to ask."

I felt a bit funny as I was the one who needed the favor, but I didn't know how else to say it.

"Earl, Conley has got himself into a peck of trouble," Ray said. "He was influenced by older teens who went joyriding. You know he is from an upstanding, hard-working family that will not countenance this behavior."

I wished Ray would talk plainly and not show off, but Earl, a heavyset, balding man in his fifties, seemed to understand.

"Would you write something about Conley that I can take to the judge showing his good character?"

Earl beamed with self-importance. That was the first time he was asked to address a judge.

Earl took the pad of paper with Earl Graves General Store printed at the top that he kept on the counter. After licking the pencil tip, he wrote a few short words in his best longhand that made me proud.

Dear Judge, Conley Ford is a good boy. I know him well. He has never been any bother. Please go easy on him. — Earl Graves, proprietor.

Ray and I also reached out to retired Pastor Peters; Carl Hall for whom I'd pitched hay, and his father Austin Hall, a retired captain in the Knox County Sheriff's Department. It made me feel good that they said I was a good kid worthy of a second chance.

That next week at my hearing at Loudon County Court, Ray made a plea for leniency that had much of the courtroom in tears. Wearing a dark suit, crisp white shirt, and blue striped tie, Ray told the story about the struggles of our family including hard times during the Depression and the move from Kentucky to Tennessee— that happened before I was born. He named each one of our siblings, pointing out that none of them had ever been in trouble with the law.

In the courtroom Ray's eyes sparkled as he spoke. Although I towered over Ray, his stature grew with each account of past events.

"Judge, I am a proud member of the Ford family— one of the biggest families in these parts. My parents, both seated here, having lost one baby, came through the Cumberland Gap with seven children to find a new life in East Tennessee," Ray said.

"Here they had eight more children, losing their youngest. They raised us with the value of hard work. While not church-going folks, my parents both know the Bible well and can quote scripture."

Ray told of our family having to move from place to place when our father, who'd been laid off from the railroad, was trying to find work.

"We used sawmill wood slabs to make chairs and a table at one homestead, and then had to burn the furniture just to keep warm."

Ray went on with that way of talking that had some in the courtroom, saying "amen" under their breath.

Looking like a well-disciplined boy with my dark hair nicely parted on the side and combed over, I wore a tucked-in, light-blue cotton shirt, brown belt, and a pair of hand-me-down khakis that were too short for me.

I took after Dad in that I was already tall, about 5 ft. 10, and was the only brown-eyed Ford son. All my brothers were short or medium in height and had Mom's blue eyes.

My parents were in the courtroom as were the owners of the Mercury we'd stolen that night in Lenoir City. Austin Hall made an impression because he came to the hearing in his sheriff department uniform.

Ray didn't make light of my involvement but pointed out that we hadn't damaged the Mercury and the only thing missing was a couple of gallons of gasoline.

"Conley is a fine boy from a big family, who has been raised on hard work and tough love." Ray waved his hands around as he wrapped up his speech.

Luckily, the police investigation didn't discover what else we did that night. I realized the other boys must've kept their mouths shut.

The other Mercurys we took weren't part of my hearing. I didn't question why, but supposed Ray worked to ensure I was only tried for one theft.

There was no jury and I didn't have to testify. The judge asked to see Ray and me in his chambers before making his ruling. The judge was tall, had gray hair, bushy white eyebrows, and wore a black robe. We sat facing the judge in two living-room chairs.

"Your Honor, my family can assure you that, going forward, my young brother here will stay out of trouble. He has learned his lesson," Ray said.

"Young man, what do you have to say for yourself?"

"Mr. Judge, I am sorry for what I did, and I know it was wrong." Ray coached me to admit guilt if asked.

"Stealing cars is a very serious matter and cannot be taken lightly. At thirteen you should've known better."

I nodded my head. I was sweating and my hands were shaking. Part of my case of nerves was due to not being completely truthful. I'd rationalized in my head we weren't really stealing cars because we didn't intend to keep them.

Behind the judge's big mahogany desk there was an empty, wooden coat-tree stand that looked like bare, outstretched arms pointing upward. It invited my eyes to drift to the ceiling where the paint was peeling. I looked down and spotted a few white chips on the rug, momentarily taking my mind off my predicament.

The judge agreed to put me on a yearlong probation and release me to my parents. I breathed a sigh of relief.

After the hearing, I overheard Ray telling Mom and Dad my record would be sealed because of my age. If

I stayed out of trouble for a year, the record would be expunged, a word I didn't understand.

I hadn't seen Roger since that day at the Loudon County Jail. I felt bad we lost touch after our brush with the law.

<hr>

My entire criminal matter from arrest to hearing took about two weeks. I was shown a writeup in the *Knoxville News Sentinel* about Detective Bunch and how he'd solved the case of the missing Mercurys. None of our names were printed because of our ages.

I hadn't been to school at all during the process. The morning I was scheduled to go back, my sister Annie went out ahead of me to the bus stop that was about a quarter mile down the hill and around the corner by Earl Graves' store.

I had on brown leather shoes with laces, blue denim Roebucks, and my favorite jacket, inherited from my brother Joe. It had two matching breast pockets with flaps. I had fifty cents in my pants pocket.

As I walked down our long driveway, I stopped in my tracks. My thoughts suddenly overcame me. My face grew red. I was still the new kid and would be called a "jailbird." The thoughts of taunts and jeers horrified me.

"They'll stare, point, and might even laugh." I shook my head.

When I reached the road, I put out my thumb, caught my first ride, and kept going.

Chapter Three

ATLANTA

Within a minute, a gray, 1950 Chevy Styleline stopped. The driver rolled down the window and said he was going as far as Merchants Road and Central Avenue Pike, an eight-minute ride at the most.

"That's exactly where I'm headed." For me, that was the first of many white lies.

"Great! Hop in."

The destination was fine, because I knew it was a good place to catch another ride. I climbed into the front seat and chatted about the pretty day.

Thoughts raced through my mind as I stared at the hilly, winding road ahead. I was on the loose: free from my police matter, school, farm work, and my domineering Dad. I took a deep breath and swore my heart skipped a beat.

After being dropped off, I crouched and made a double-knot in the pesky shoelace that almost got stuck in the car door. A dry wind had picked up so I pulled out my pocket comb and smoothed my hair before looking for another ride.

Since the move to Dry Gap Pike, I'd become an expert hitchhiker. The rules I picked up were simple. We had to be halfway presentable, stand in an area where there was plenty room for a car to pull over, and always face the traffic, with arm extended and thumb out. We asked the driver how far they were going and didn't accept the ride unless they were going most, if not all, of the way to our stop. We were polite and remembered to say "thank you," even when turning down a ride. There was an unwritten rule among hitchhiking boys that if word got out, we were ungrateful or rude, motorists would pass us by.

I walked to the traffic light in Inskip where I caught another ride, passing through my old neighborhood. I got out at the Park National Bank at the corner of Broadway and Central where Dad deposited his paychecks.

I walked briskly south on Broadway passing the City Jail where I'd been held after my arrest and the telephone office where two of my sisters worked. I then passed by the L&N Railroad Depot where Dad worked.

The Depot reminded me of the day when I was about five years old and Dad took me to the freight office. I climbed onto the bridge over the tracks to wait for a steam engine on its way to the roundhouse.

When the engine passed below, a long burst of steam saturating me with black soot blew straight up from the locomotive's chimney. The more I rubbed my face, the worse it got.

When I climbed down, the black men working on the loading platform were tickled seeing how black I was. They laughed out loud at this "young'un." Dad got on my case but later made jokes about it, making me feel stupid. My face got red when I thought about the laughs Dad got at my expense.

To stop that line of thought, I repeated: "go, go, go!" I sung them over and over in my head to the "do-rae-mi" musical scale.

"I'll head south where it's always warm," I thought, shrugging off any doubts. "I'll go to Florida and get me some oranges. What the heck—I can live on orange juice."

Although I hadn't filled out and didn't shave, I was tall for my age and could pass for sixteen.

Shit, I was a city boy turned farm-hand who knew how to work hard and make a buck. What else could happen? At thirteen, I'd already been arrested, could castrate a boar, hot wire a car, and take care of myself.

From the L&N Depot, I hiked up Cumberland Avenue by the administration building at the University of Tennessee. Although I had to walk more than intended, I managed to hitch a couple of rides on the Alcoa Highway just past the airport to Maryville where I picked up the two-lane U.S. Highway 411 toward Georgia.

From Maryville, I hitched to Vonore to Etowah to Ocoee, all along 411. I always asked how far they were going and to let me out in a spot where there was room to pull over so I could catch another ride. Sometimes it took a while. I got short rides from individuals or couples. Sometimes I rode in the front seat and sometimes in the back. Most motorists were hospitable.

While still in Tennessee when people asked where I was headed, I named the next big town.

On one ride, I sat in the back next to a chubby, freckle-faced, six-year-old boy. He gave me an Atomic Fire Ball jawbreaker from his Roy Rogers lunchbox that set my mouth on fire. When I flinched and used my hand to fan my mouth, the kid couldn't stop laughing. Some of his spit squirted out between his missing front teeth, landing on my jacket. I was happy to be let out and see that family pull away.

Small talk came naturally to me, honed from all the door-to-door peddling I'd done when we lived on Scott Avenue. My conversation wasn't limited to weather. I could talk about cows, goats, tomatoes, corn, hay, snakes, quail hunting and catching bluegill at Norris Lake.

No one ever asked about book learning, which was fine with me. My best use of a schoolbook had been strapping it onto an old roller-skate and careening down the street on my butt with my legs extended.

Having eaten nothing since breakfast, I bought a packet of peanut butter crackers for a nickel at a country store in Etowah. My hands shook as I ripped open the wrapper and stuffed the crackers into my mouth two at a time. I used the bathroom and craning my neck under the faucet, took a long, cool drink before getting back on the road.

It was late afternoon when I arrived in Ocoee, which is about ten miles from the Georgia state line.

I wondered, "God, what am I gonna do?" when a green Oldsmobile Rocket 88 with Tennessee plates stopped.

"I'm going to Atlanta," I told the driver, a man in his twenties. I guessed he was a paint salesman from the stack of colorful paint brochures on the backseat.

"You're in luck, I'm going all the way to Atlanta and would enjoy the company," he said in a west Tennessee drawl unlike the hillbilly twang I was used to. He introduced himself as Jerry and said he was on his way to a sales conference.

As we pulled away, Jerry turned the radio dial to a Dragnet rerun, a signal he wasn't looking for conversation. I stretched, yawned, and struggled to keep my eyes open before nodding off.

It was dark when we pulled into a truck stop with a small cafe in Chatsworth, about thirty minutes inside Georgia. We grabbed two stools at Doyle's.

With only forty-five cents in my pocket, I ordered coffee and upended the glass sugar dispenser to pour a ton of the sweet stuff into my cup before slurping some down.

"Aren't you hungry?" Jerry asked.

"I'm okay."

He saw me looking longingly at the pecan pie sitting under a glass dome on the counter.

"You go ahead and order something, and I'll pay for it."

I ordered a grilled cheese sandwich that came with two huge cucumber-size pickles. The cafe offered free coffee refills.

"Think you've got enough sugar in there?" the waitress asked as she refilled my cup. I also scarfed down a piece of that pecan pie, which was about the best I'd ever tasted.

Jerry was interested in my reasons for going south.

"I had to quit school to work on our family farm outside Knoxville. Then last week my uncle came down sick. He lives in Atlanta and needs my help around the house." I surprised myself at how believable that sounded.

I told him my name was Joe Ford. My brother Joe was about four years older than me and I knew his story, like the fact he worked in a grocery store. If I told anyone my real age, I figured they'd dump me in a minute.

Jerry nodded and told me he'd been married a year. He had a baby son named Cecil, they called Cricket because he chirped rather than cried. He showed me the kid's picture in his wallet while pulling out a five-dollar bill. He told our waitress to keep the change.

The cafe had free aluminum ashtrays engraved with Doyle's. I grabbed one on my way out. It fit perfectly in my pants pocket.

While driving the ninety miles to Atlanta, Jerry turned on an episode of the radio crime serial Perry Mason that helped pass the time. We stopped about halfway for gas in Cartersville. Then it was on through Marietta, arriving in Atlanta around 10 p.m. Jerry let me out on Peachtree Street by the Varsity restaurant near Georgia Tech.

"Are you sure you're okay?"

"Yup! Thanks so much. Much obliged for the meal and ride." Tired and jumpy, I accidentally slammed the passenger-side door too hard. But Jerry just smiled and waved as he drove off.

It was too late to go any farther that night. As a horde of people roamed around me, I stood on the brightly lit sidewalk in the midst of a jumble of noisy traffic and multi-colored neon signs. The rotten-eggs smell of exhaust hung in the night air. Looking around made me feel dizzy, like I was inside a spinning top with the world whizzing around outside. I stamped by feet to make the sensation stop.

I'd just been let off in the biggest city in the South after dark, where I didn't know a single soul. What was I going to do now? I took a deep breath, got my wits about me, and tried to compose myself. The need to find food and a place to sleep helped me focus.

I spotted an attractive woman with a friendly face, who looked like my sister Betty, and asked her for directions to the Greyhound bus station. I thought I'd hang out there until morning. As it turned out, the bus station was just a few blocks away. Before I got underway, the Varsity restaurant caught my eye.

When telling stories about his days on the road looking for work during the Depression, Dad said he'd stop at the best restaurant in town—one that could afford to feed him. He'd offer to work for a meal but often a big-hearted waitress would take care of him, paying for the meal out of her own pocket.

I discovered the Varsity was cafeteria-style and I wouldn't have to approach a waitress. There were leftovers on the tables, as well as bottles of ketchup and sugar on the condiment counter.

Helping myself to a half-eaten hamburger and some cold fries from a table, I put some sugar in a paper napkin to take with me.

I walked around and came across Piedmont Park where an unshaven and disheveled man, stinking of alcohol, approached me. Drunks were commonplace in Happy Holler that was a block from our old house on East Scott. I knew they were unpredictable and best avoided.

One of the Holler's regulars, Rooster Hunter, standing about six-foot, four-inches and weighing 250 pounds, was awfully bad when drunk. He used his huge hands, callused from a life of work as a railroad laborer, to clobber anyone who looked at him crosswise. Even the police wouldn't take Rooster on. They'd wait for him to wear himself out fighting before taking him in to sober up.

Rooster's rule over the Holler changed one summer evening when John Fogarty, owner of Fogarty Jewelers—had enough of the ruckus near his store. He challenged Rooster to quiet things down. As a crowd gathered, the two had words.

"Rooster, it's high time to put a lid on this racket," said Mr. Fogarty, whose voice was surprisingly strong for a small man. He was about six inches shorter and 100 pounds lighter than Rooster.

"Whaddya say?" Rooster said as he turned around. He patted the top of Mr. Fogarty's head, and stared down at him with his mostly toothless grin apart from a snaggletooth. "Whaddya say, little John?"

Mr. Fogarty didn't say a word before smacking Rooster right under the jawbone. The perfectly placed punch knocked Rooster right off his feet. Until then, we had no idea Mr. Fogarty, who was always dressed like a businessman, had been an amateur boxer in his youth.

<hr>

I left Piedmont Park but the drunk followed me to the bus station where I looked around for cover. I sat down next to a young boy with his mother. They were headed to Chattanooga. I told them I was from Tennessee but was going to visit family in Florida. The three of us chatted until their bus was called around 1 a.m. By that time, the drunk had gone on his way.

Finding a quiet spot in the back of the lobby between the lockers, I sat down and dozed off for about an hour. Waking up with a chill and a crick in my neck, I got to thinking it wasn't the best place to spend the rest of the night.

I went outside and found a rectangular stoop that jutted out several feet from the foundation of the building in a utility area where the buses lined up. Hugging my legs, I wadded up my jacket to use as a pillow. Too tired to dream, I slept for a couple of hours. The public address system, announcing arrival and departure times for Columbus, Charlotte, and Roanoke, woke me up at daylight.

I cleaned up by wetting a bunch of paper towels to wipe my face in the restroom. The toilet stalls cost a nickel so I crawled underneath the door to take a crap. At the bus station counter, I bought a dime's worth of hard candy.

After studying the map on the bus station wall to pick the best route out of Atlanta, I walked along Peachtree Street, asking passersby to point me in the right direction.

It was too early for breakfast at the Varsity that was open just for coffee. After buying a cup of coffee for a nickel, I loaded up a napkin with relish and ketchup before heading out.

It still took me the better part of the morning with a combination of walking and hitchhiking to get out of Atlanta. Once I reached U.S. Highway 23, I hitched a number of rides to Jackson, arriving around noontime.

Sometimes my rides offered me nourishment such as an apple or a piece of candy and water from a thermos. For energy between rides, I wet my fingers and alternated dipping them in the sugar, ketchup, and relish that I'd wrapped in paper napkins.

I hooked up with a dozen or so short rides by the time I reached Macon. When darkness crept in, I walked along the highway in a small town a few miles south of

Macon. I spotted an old barn on the side of the road. I thought the barn would have hay inside providing me with a comfortable spot to sleep and get away from the dampness of the humid night. There was no hay, but I crawled onto the loft anyway and sat in the corner hugging myself with my arms.

I was getting closer to Florida and repeated the word Florida over and over in my head, again stressing the last syllable: Flor-i-*da*. It sounded upbeat. Like counting sheep. The repetition helped me fall asleep.

In my dream, my mind wandered to Black Oak Ridge, a scraggy hillside farm that Dad used as a workcamp for my brothers and me.

My brother David and I had the grimy job of collecting slop for our hogs at Black Oak Ridge on the way to the Oakwood grade school each day. We dug deeply into the garbage barrels in the alleyways behind houses and apartments along our route. We filled five-gallon tin paint buckets with any food scraps like stale bread, lettuce, apple cores, potato peelings, and eggshells. We were ashamed of this chore and avoided houses where our schoolmates lived. At times it was disgusting as we would have to sort through wet, drippy flour gravy or even used Kotex.

Upon arrival at school, David and I had a secret spot by the boiler room outside Oakwood where we'd hide our buckets during the school day. We washed our hands in the semicircle-shaped, foot-pedal sink outside the bathrooms on the first floor.

We often had waist-level stains on our shirts from bending over into the rusty fifty-five-gallon rubbish barrels. When other pupils noticed, we couldn't admit to rifling through garbage. We said we'd taken out the coal ash from the furnace before heading to school.

<hr />

At daylight, awoken by the sound of trucks speeding by, I collected myself, stretched and glanced outside. I spotted a full-grown pecan tree by the side of the road.

When I got out, I shuffled through the leaves by the tree with my right foot and kicked up a pecan. "Wow, this is great—like finding buried treasure." I found several handfuls and filled my jacket pockets. I easily cracked their thin shells by putting two nuts in my right hand, making a fist, and squeezing it with my left.

I caught various rides along Highway 23 and by midafternoon, I reached the outskirts of Waycross, Georgia that was about seventy-five miles from Jacksonville, Florida.

It was extremely hot and humid. I stripped off the light jacket I'd put on for school two days earlier and bundled it up under my left arm.

Along the road, pine trees with buckets attached collected sap that I later found out was used to make turpentine. There were also miles of fields that still had a few white fluffy cotton balls that pickers had missed. Being an East Tennessean, I was familiar with tobacco, feed corn, and hay crops, but I'd never seen a cotton field. Along the edges of the fields were more pecan trees.

As I was thumbing for a ride and munching on the pecans in Waycross—a new, baby-blue Buick convertible pulled up with the white ragtop down. The car had temporary Vermont plates made out of cardboard. The only thing I knew about Vermont, was it was a state somewhere up north.

I introduced myself as Joe Ford and said I was headed to Florida.

There was nothing unusual about Al, the man who was driving, except he had a northern accent and spoke like a radio announcer. I guessed he was around thirty-five years old; he had a medium build, wore a short-sleeve shirt, dress pants, and straw fedora.

Ernie, the passenger, was around fifty and had on work clothes. He said he'd be the next one getting out and moved to the back seat. Ernie was another hitchhiker and was headed to St. Augustine. Al was some kind of draftsman by trade and despite being a Yankee, he played country music nonstop on the radio.

They had bread, sandwich meat, soft drinks, and even some cookies. Having a dry mouth from the pecans, I accepted a Coca-Cola right off even though it was warm.

I told them I had some "PEE-cans" and Al asked what those were. I pulled some out of my pocket and he laughed.

"Oh, you mean pee-CAANS!"

Riding in a convertible with the top down going south, I was as close to being in heaven as I could imagine. I started to relax with thoughts of home, school, and family now in the rearview mirror as the country song "Live Fast, Love Hard, Die Young," by Faron Young played on the radio.

I felt the setting sun on my forehead and warm wind in my face. The time flew by and in roughly thirty-five miles, we crossed the state line into Florida. I swear I could smell the Atlantic Ocean before getting my first glimpse of the bluest water and whitest sand I'd ever seen.

On the other side of Jacksonville, we took a detour off coastal U.S. Highway One and turned inland for about five minutes into an unpopulated area where we found a dirt path leading into an orange grove. Al drove the Buick right into the grove where he said we would spend the night among the trees.

I was surprised to see the oranges were mostly green. And one of the trees had a small, funny looking fruit on it called kumquats. Al and Ernie laughed at me when I tried to peel a kumquat telling me to eat the whole thing. So, I took a big bite wincing from the bitter taste that caused them to laugh even more.

It must have been around 10 p.m. when Al put the top up so the three of us could get some shuteye. I got positioned to sleep, sitting up and resting against the passenger door. I realized why Ernie had wanted the backseat so he could stretch out. A lightning bug caught my eye and I reached out the window to grab it and missed.

My buddies and I dreamed of getting rich by collecting lightning bugs on Scott Avenue. My sister Ethel worked at Oak Ridge, nicknamed Atomic City, and through her, we heard that Oak Ridge would pay big bucks for the bugs for research on the atomic bomb. We thought lightning bugs were a new weapon important to the defense of the country.

Around dusk, there was nothing quite like chasing after a lightning bug and grabbing it in my hand. It was amazing to see fifty bugs all light up at the same time in a mason jar but the sad thing was, the next morning, all their lights were burned out.

I remember late one summer night waking up in a sweat with my heart pounding and picking up the mason jar from beside my bed. The dead bugs were piled up in near-total darkness with the exception of a single, lonely lightning bug that was still trying to glow.

For some reason, I was overcome with the desire to save it. So, I jumped out of bed in the basement sleeping area—that I shared with my brothers Joe and David—my bare feet slipping on the dirt floor. I charged up the steps and out the front door onto the porch where I opened the lid to the jar to let the lightning bug out.

With freedom soon at hand, the tiny insect didn't seem to know what to do. It hesitated on the rim of the jar, turned and gave me a look, and then flew off into the night with its light glowing brighter as it picked up speed.

I now felt like that lonely lightning bug. Not sure where I was headed or why—but, on my way, nevertheless.

∞∞∞∞∞∞∞∞∞∞∞∞∞∞∞∞∞∞∞∞∞∞∞∞∞∞∞∞∞∞∞∞∞

Despite Ernie's snoring—that was peaceful and reassuring—I shut my eyes and finally got some badly needed rest.

We started early the next morning, stopping at a gas station where we cleaned up a little bit. I noticed that Al brought a shaving kit with him into the restroom. When he came out, he looked neat and well-groomed.

Although we had some oranges in the car, we spotted a big billboard on Highway One that advertised all the orange juice you could drink for ten cents. Al slowed down to pull into the highway farm stand where fresh-squeezed orange juice was in huge containers with self-help spigots. I paid a dime, got a cup and with the juice spilling onto my jaw, drank half-a-gallon in less than ten minutes. It tasted every bit as sweet as I'd imagined.

Chapter Four

FLORIDA

With the thermometer reaching the mid-eighties, Al put the top down as we made our way to St. Augustine along US Highway One. With acres of cloudless blue sky, Florida was turning out to be everything I'd hoped. I didn't own a pair of shades so I squinted, but I didn't care. The sun on my forehead and forearms felt great.

Al pulled over by the Ponce de Leon Hotel that looked like a massive castle. Fountains everywhere of different sizes sprouted water that reflected like a million tiny mirrors in the sunlight. St. Augustine was nothing like home. The wide, tree-lined streets were called boulevards. We had a few boulevards in Knoxville, but they were plain in comparison. Here, huge palm trees hugged both the sides of the road.

Ernie said his friends in the city would put him up until he could find work. I felt a pang of sadness as Ernie walked down the boulevard with his small, tattered travel bag.

Goodbyes were always hard for me. When my oldest siblings visited with their children, I begged them to take me with them. They knew life for a kid at home was rough—they'd been through it themselves. But with grown-up problems of their own, they always left me behind. When I was really small, I'd run down the street after them with tears streaming down my face. But as time went on, I'd hide in the back alley with my back up against a tree where no one could see me cry.

Al spent time driving around neighborhoods where I was amazed to see pink houses with orange tile roofs. He wrote house numbers down in a notebook, jotting down if a number was 126 Cypress Dr., for example, and the next house was 130.

Seeing a little girl on Cypress Drive trying to ride her two-wheeler brought a smile to my face. I remembered my sister Annie struggling to stay upright on her first ride on an old bicycle.

"Little Robert" Van Winkle lived just three doors away from us in the Peters Apartments. He often came to our house to make music with our tenant Don Williams who, with his twin brother Bob, made up the "Two Religious Singers." The twins performed at churches around the city.

A regular on Cas Walker's radio show, Little Robert was a popular country singer and picker. Standing only thirty-nine inches tall due to his short legs, Little Robert—who was always well dressed—looked completely normal apart from his height. When performing, he had to climb onto a wooden apple crate to reach the microphone.

One day, Little Robert showed me the inside of his flashy, Nassau-blue-metallic Cadillac. The gas and brake pedals had been extended so his feet could reach them. All the boys on the street admired his car and I felt special being shown the interior workings.

But Little Robert's sunny disposition was tested when Annie rode her bike into his Cadillac parked on the side of Scott Avenue. She put a big dent in the driver's side door.

He strode down to our house to check on Annie and ask for the repair costs. Apart from a scratch on her knee, Annie was fine and was sitting on the bike on the sidewalk when Little Robert arrived.

Dad was on the porch and walked down the front steps to greet him.

"Mr. Ford, I'm relieved to see your daughter wasn't badly hurt," said Little Robert, with his arms folded and in a deep-toned voice despite his small size. "But I respectfully ask that you pay to repair the damage to my car door."

Little Robert looked straight up at my Dad, who stood six feet tall but seemed taller. I admired his nerve.

But he didn't get very far; in a curt manner, Dad told him to talk to his insurance company.

"That's what insurance is for. Now you have a nice day." Dad turned around and walked up the front steps.

Little Robert did an about face and walked as briskly as his little legs could take him. The altercation didn't deter him from coming back to our house to sing with the Williams twins.

A few months later Little Robert had to crawl out the window when his Cadillac rolled over in an accident. A woman, passing by, nearly fainted saying, *Lordy, that man's lost his legs!* Cas Walker repeated that story many times on the radio when Little Robert was his guest.

<hr />

After driving around, Al stopped at a small corner store that didn't look much different than the ones at home. He wrote a check out to Joe Ford for nine dollars and instructed me to go inside and pick out some groceries that added up to around three dollars. I'd pay with the check and bring back the change. He told me if they asked for an address to use the "missing address" 128 Cypress Dr.

Al then briefed me on what I should say: I was picking up a few things for my mother with the check I got for doing yard work for a neighbor. Al's printing on the check looked very neat.

"What if I'm asked a bunch of questions and goof up?"

"Don't worry about it. Since it's my check, you're not doing anything wrong. If they don't accept it, just say 'thank you' and leave." Al parked a block away.

Because I was young, had a southern accent, and looked like an honest kid, Al said I'd get away with it. I knew what we were doing was wrong because I might have to lie—but that didn't stop me. I can't explain it other than I'd already broken the law and this didn't seem like that big a deal. Also, with Al taking responsibility, I thought I was in the clear.

I went inside and bought a box of Tide detergent, a two-pound bag of pinto beans, and a package of

Marshmallow sandwich cookies. The total came to $1.50 and to my surprise, the cute teenage clerk was trusting and didn't ask any questions. She told me to sign the back of the check, stamped it, and counted out the change. Her name tag said Mae. I noticed a silver charm bracelet with a tiny alligator on her wrist.

"Much obliged, Mae," I replied with a small grin and stuffed the change into my pocket. "By the way, Mae is my Mom's middle name."

"Y'all come back soon," she said with a shy smile.

"See you later alligator!" I replied.

I left thinking I had a knack for this.

When I gave Al the $7.50 in change, he asked why I bought stuff we couldn't eat.

"I figured no one could argue with a boy buying washing powder for his mother," I said.

Al smiled and nodded his head. Those pinto beans and box of Tide stayed in the car the entire time I was traveling with Al.

When I told him about the clerk, he cautioned me not to get too friendly.

"You want to be forgettable," he said.

We continued along the coastal highway reaching Daytona Beach after stopping at several small stores. Each time, I cashed a check for a little bit more—but never more than twenty dollars.

Al decided to look for stores with two or more counters rather than a small "mom & pop" store because the owner wasn't likely to be one of the cashiers.

We cashed checks all the way to Fort Lauderdale. Al gave me a dollar each time. The stores were full of Halloween candy and displays.

One time, the young girl in my checkout asked the other cashier to approve the check. I smiled as best I could and swallowed hard as he sized me up for a couple of seconds before nodding his approval.

In Fort Lauderdale, Al answered a newspaper advertisement for a job at a local engineering company. While he was inside, I got out of the car to scout around and found a coconut resting under a palm tree in the front yard of a house. I picked it up and shook it near my ear. I decided to keep it and crack it open later to eat.

"Hey you, young man!" yelled a woman who threw open the front door. She waved her arms around and screamed at me. "Put that coconut down right this minute or I'll call the police! That's part of my landscaping display!"

I returned it to the spot in her garden, shrugged, waved apologetically, and quickly walked away.

At a local bank in Fort Lauderdale, Al opened an account and obtained another book of blank checks. We stopped at small grocery stores on the way to Miami where Al applied for another job, went to another bank, and got more blank checks.

Al decided we'd spend the night in a beach parking lot by a fishing pier that jutted out into the ocean. A lot of people milled about, so there was little chance of a police officer questioning why we were there.

While Al was having a beer at a local bar, I went for a walk on the pier where there was a peddler selling soft drinks out of a cooler. I bought an ice-cold Coca-Cola. I removed my shoes and socks and took a stroll on the beach, putting my toes in the white sand and wading in the Atlantic Ocean for the first time in my life. The water was surprisingly warm. I reached down with my Doyle's ashtray to get a little water and tasted it with my tongue. It was salty! So different from the lakes and muddy swimming holes I was used to.

A lame dog that looked like a beagle mix wandered up to me. I cracked a couple of pecans for him. He licked my bare toes as a thank you.

I briefly wondered if anyone missed me at home. If I missed anyone, it was my sister Betty. I didn't miss my Dad. His mean streak included hurting dogs.

<hr>

I saw Dad kick Fido in the groin on Scott Avenue, sending him squealing home, because the big mutt peed on a shrub in front of our house at the same time every day. He was sick of it.

Fido was a nice dog, loved by all us kids. I wanted to call Fido back, give him a hug, and say it was going to be okay. But I knew that would make Dad even madder.

Fido's owner Dewey Jackson, who was the chaplain with the Knoxville police, called the law. Soon, three police cars showed up drawing a crowd and causing a local hullabaloo.

It wasn't clear what was said between Dad and the patrolmen. The entire police matter took about fifteen minutes and Dad didn't discuss it. Likely, Dad did his best to explain his side of things but with Dewey's connection, knew better than to argue with the cops.

The incident ended any neighborliness between the Fords and the Jacksons.

At daylight Al and I cleaned up in the public restroom and started driving across Florida on U.S. Highway 41 toward Naples and Fort Myers with plans to head up the west coast. It was the start of my fifth day on the road.

With Webb Pierce singing, "In the Jailhouse Now" on the radio, we continued along using the same "m.o.," cashing checks all the way up past Tampa. In Sarasota, Al decided we could buy a set of tires and make some serious money selling them.

When we stopped at an auto tire store, I did my best with the salesman, saying we needed a set of tires. I introduced Al as my uncle who would pay for them by check. I said I wanted a full set of black-wall, fifteen-inch tires. But the salesman kept asking more questions, which I couldn't easily answer.

Al got a bad feeling and decided to abandon the plan. So as soon as the salesman stepped away to see what tires he had, Al said, "let's go." We walked out and drove off.

It was getting dark as we headed north and the roads were poorly lit. We were traveling along at a good clip when the roadway suddenly forked and Al hit a low concrete island.

"Damn!" Al exclaimed and pulled over.

I crawled under the edge of the car, but it was too dark to see if there was any damage.

Soon it was apparent the oil pan was leaking. Oil blew onto the hot muffler and tailpipe as we drove along, so the smoky smell was pretty overpowering. We had to stop several times to add oil and bought the cheapest available. Al was really concerned because the mechanical situation could draw attention to us. He didn't want to be pulled over by the cops.

After about an hour, we found a service station where the attendant was still on site but there was no mechanic on duty. Al convinced the young man to let him to use the lube-and-oil rack.

Once the car was raised, Al found that the oil pan drain plug was damaged. Before he started working on the car, he put his dress watch on the workbench.

I watched from the garage entrance as Al made a temporary fix. He put sealant around the plug, covered it with an old rag, and secured it with a piece of wire. He wiped off the excess oil that coated the underside of the car.

When the work was done, Al lowered the car and checked the dip stick, adding four quarts of oil. With another rag, Al cleaned his hands and forearms as best he could.

"I'm really strapped for cash and hope this isn't too expensive," Al said.

From the way the attendant was listening, I guessed he was understanding.

"I've gotta charge you for the oil. Use of the rack is free," he said.

Al pulled out a couple of dollars from his wallet and some change from his pocket. He turned around to get his watch.

"Here, this is for you. You did so much to help me, I want you to have my watch," he said.

"You don't have to do that," the attendant replied.

"I insist."

The attendant admired the watch for a few seconds before putting it on his wrist.

Al's face didn't show whether he was upset about parting with his prize watch with calfskin strap.

He told me he had it in his mind all along to give the attendant his watch because he couldn't write him a check. If he had, once the check bounced, the attendant could identify him and the car.

We got back into the car and headed toward the Florida panhandle.

Around 11 p.m. that same night, Al pulled over at a roadside honky-tonk and went inside to have a beer while I drifted off in the car. A policeman gave me a start when he tapped on the window.

"Are you okay, son?" As he shone his flashlight in my face.

"I'm good. My uncle is inside."

"Just checking." The policeman wandered away, inspecting the other cars. Thankfully, he didn't notice the temporary Vermont tags.

I slept as Al drove through the night, reaching Mobile, Alabama and then Biloxi, Mississippi in the morning where we gassed up. Biloxi was the place where my brother Bill had been hospitalized at Kessler Air Force Base. The base was on one side of the road with the Gulf of Mexico on the other side with even whiter sand than in Miami.

Exhausted from driving all night, Al pulled over and took a snooze on a park bench overlooking the Gulf. I spent the time clearing trash from inside the car. I thought about Bill's mental illness and how the entire focus of my family had turned to Bill when I needed attention the most.

Just a month before my twelfth birthday, Bill—who was eleven years older than me—came home for Christmas on a short leave. He looked great in his blue wool Air Force uniform reflected in his sparkling blue eyes. He showed off the special zipper he'd sewn on the inner side of his calf-high, black leather boots so he didn't have to undo the laces.

Bill let me try his boots on and work the zipper. My feet were as big as his and they fit me perfectly. I marched around for ten minutes and practiced a few salutes.

"Don't you look sharp," Bill said, grinning broadly. "Connie, I have a feeling you will be in the Air Force one day."

Bill's remark caught me off guard. Could there be life after Scott Avenue for me too?

The Air Force sent Bill to cook-and-baker's school because of his experience working at Merita Bakery and the fish market in Knoxville. He was assigned as a meat cutter at the base commissary and had been promoted to Airman First Class.

Although Bill had Dad's black hair, he was like mother with his easygoing personality, warm smile, and kind heart. He spent most of his time at home that Christmas with his girlfriend, Dorothy Dempsey, who lived just two doors away. Dorothy was pretty and so slender that she looked like Popeye's girlfriend Olive Oil when she stood next to Bill, who was a lot shorter than she was.

After the holidays, Bill returned to Ramey Air Force Base in Puerto Rico where he was stationed.

About a month later, the Air Force called with the news Bill had been moved to the base hospital. We huddled around the black, rotary desk telephone in the foyer when Bill was put on the line. He didn't sound right.

"Hey Bill, how ya doin'?" I said into the receiver.

But Bill kept repeating over and over, "You gotta be my baby brother; you gotta be my baby brother." I handed the phone back to Mom.

Bill's call left me with an odd feeling. I knew we were both well aware of who I was and my position in the family.

"Bill was not himself," Dad said curtly, being the last one to speak to Bill. None of us dwelled on the episode. We brushed it off assuming he was running a fever from some sort of illness.

But a few weeks later we got a call from Air Force doctors at the hospital at Kessler Air Force Base where

Bill had been moved. They said Bill was unresponsive, describing his condition as schizophrenia, an illness that we'd never heard of, nor understood.

The Air Force told Dad they were not aware of any triggering event that could've caused his mental break. They said he'd already received a series of electric shock treatments.

My brother Henry, who by that time had completed his military service and was working for the railroad in Indiana, came home to drive Mom and Dad to Biloxi. They packed a small, brown leather suitcase between them. Mom wore her navy-blue rayon dress with lace collar and mother-of-pearl buttons, that was only used for weddings and funerals. She put on her hat and white gloves for the trip.

Dad donned a brown suitcoat that was worn in places, one of two pairs of khaki pants he owned, an old yellowing white shirt, and a brown fedora. Apart from Henry's wedding, it was first time I'd seen Dad wear a necktie.

Henry and our parents headed southwest in our old Ford sedan for the nearly twelve-hour drive. It was the farthest away from home that Mom had ever traveled.

At the base hospital, Dad had a real "Ford fit"—a temper tantrum peculiar to my family that comes from a deep, dark place. He wouldn't accept Bill's diagnosis and was adamant that Bill would snap out of it once he was home. Scary when in a rage, Dad made such a scene at the hospital that the doctors wrote in their official report that Airman Ford's father was also mentally ill.

Dad insisted Bill be stationed at home. About three months later, Bill came back to Knoxville and was awarded a rating of thirty percent for medical disability. Dad refused to let the Air Force rate him at 100 percent because it would stigmatize him. The Air Force sent him a small monthly check for the rest of his life.

Bill's once vibrant and engaging blue eyes, now appeared vacant, staring off into some distant place. He never smiled unless he was laughing to himself. Sometimes his lips would move and nothing would come out. If we told Bill to raise his arm, he would raise it and leave it up there until told to put it down. He mostly sat quietly and smoked continuously. Once he finished a cigarette, he lighted another one up.

To get Bill out of bed and keep him busy, Dad called in a favor and got him a job at Cathy's Appliance on Clinton Highway where we'd purchased a washing machine and our TV. Bill couldn't handle interacting with people so that job lasted only one day.

Then Dad paid Hank Price a small amount to let Bill "work" at his hardware store. Bill didn't do any real work, but Hank let him sit by idly and it provided Bill a place to go.

Bill's girlfriend Dorothy visited almost daily in those first few weeks. Heartbroken, she eventually moved on without Bill.

Some months later, Mom and Dad put Bill in the East Tennessee State Hospital at Lyon's View for treatment. After one week, I accompanied them to Lyon's View to see Bill.

We signed in and an orderly took us up to Bill's ward where there were about twenty patients wearing pajamas. Some were making guttural sounds, while others shuffled up to us singing or yelling, making me feel strange.

The orderly collected Bill and we went to a visiting area. Bill was totally distant, barely acknowledging our presence. I looked right at him and said "Hey, Bill—what's up?" but he didn't answer.

Mom cried all the way home. Dad called my brother Ray and told him we had to get Bill out of there. Within a few days, Bill was back on Scott Avenue. Not long after that, Dad made plans to get Bill out of the city and move to Halls Crossroads.

Al and I finished a breakfast of eggs, biscuits, sausage, and flour gravy at a local café. Saying we were taking too many chances, he planned to go to farther west and told me he would leave me off in New Orleans. Although we'd exchanged a few stories, I didn't know anything about Al and I didn't ask questions. Yet, I was a little sad about never seeing him again.

My "family" had become everyone I came in contact with, whether it was the kids I grew up with on Scott Avenue; the Mercury Gang; the characters in Happy Holler; or people who gave me odd jobs. Even someone like Al seemed like family for a time.

As we drove the roughly two hours to New Orleans, arriving mid-afternoon, Al said he was heading to Texas. He let me out at the corner of St. Charles and Canal streets. I grabbed my jacket from the backseat; I had about fourteen dollars Al had let me keep from cashing checks.

It was Saturday and my sixth day away from home. I hadn't given any thought about what my next move would be. Going home was not an option. In my heart, I didn't believe anyone at home really cared where I was.

My sisters and brothers couldn't wait to get away. Seeing them bail out one by one and then sharing their stories of their new lives had a huge influence on me.

At home there was always a racket going on. Dad had stomach problems and battled severe psoriasis that made his skin raw. Bill was sick. Lack of money was always an issue. Having to work like a mule also contributed to creating a hardness in me.

"No, I am better off here," I mumbled.

Chapter Five

NEW ORLEANS

With my jacket slung over my shoulder, I walked about a block along St. Charles Avenue, sat down on a bench, and took a deep breath. The blue sky was cloudless. I guessed the temperature to be around eighty degrees.

I'd only been away from home for six days but it felt like eons. The Mercury Gang and being arrested were in the rearview mirror.

New Orleans was as good a place as any to stopover. There were lots of people milling about. I wasn't homesick but making connections to things I knew gave me comfort. Railroad whistles and the clang-clang of streetcars reminded me of Knoxville.

Twice, I counted up the fourteen singles I had, before folding the bills tightly, and stuffing them back into the watch pocket of my blue denims.

I'd sold tons of things door-to-door for as long as I could remember, so the prospect of getting a job didn't worry me. People were always telling Dad how hardworking his kids were. We were skilled peddlers in and around the old neighborhood, that's for sure.

Dad was a clerk at the railroad freight office and bid on goods damaged in handling or transport. When he got a deal on several dozen cases of sweet pickles that contained some broken jars, he had them delivered to the front yard. We emptied the cases, tossed the broken jars, wiped off any pickle juice, and sold them for twenty-five cents.

Another time, Dad had several cases of a gritty hand soap that came in yellow tins dropped off at the house. The paste-like soap was for people like mechanics who worked with their hands. When there was nothing else to sell, we went to homes and businesses and sold the tins for twenty-five cents apiece. It took us about two years to sell all the soap.

At one point, Dad had four coal-oil stoves, each with three burners, that had been slightly damaged in transit delivered. The small stoves on metal stands were good for apartments. They briefly set on our front porch with a sign offering them for fifteen dollars each.

Even with us kids bringing money home, Dad never stopped looking for more income. On Sundays from late July to early November, we drove to Dean Planter's Tobacco Warehouse in Knoxville, which opened its doors to farmers selling food crops during the harvest season.

Dad, who understood the produce industry from his boyhood in Kentucky at his father's store, knew how to bargain and drove our car right into the warehouse.

The farmers sold most of their supply to local grocery stores and didn't want to haul anything that was left back to their farms.

Annie, David, and I went with Dad on these trips and watched him making deals for tomatoes, potatoes, green beans, peaches, apples, or sweet corn.

Most of the time, the farmer agreed to unload the excess produce onto our front yard on his way home. But on one trip to the market, Dad negotiated a sale for what seemed like a ton of unsold tomatoes.

"Mr. L. J. Ford, I can't take time to unload these at your house. You'll have to take 'em now or leave 'em," the farmer said, spitting out a wad of tobacco on the straw-covered floor.

"I'll take them here and now," Dad said. He reached into his pants pocket and pulled out several dollar bills. The money changed hands and they shook on it.

The farmer filled the trunk of our sedan first and then poured all the remaining tomatoes through the window into the backseat. So, there we sat, up to our eyeballs in the fruit for the trip home.

Sitting between them, I looked over, first to Annie, and then to David, seeing their wide eyes just above the sea of tomatoes. We got home and slid out of the back seat along with the tomatoes, divided them up into empty one-gallon lard buckets and sold them door-to-door for twenty-five cents a gallon.

By the time the sun had set, we'd made Dad's money back, a small profit, and still had enough tomatoes for our table.

While I'd rather be hanging out with my buddies, hard work had its bright points. Food always tasted better when I was tired out from a long day. Sleep came easily on days like that.

One of my best neighborhood customers was Mrs. Price, who lived with her middle-aged son Hank on N. Central at the foot of Scott Avenue. I never knew what happened to Mr. Price, as neighbors gossiped, he went West. I considered it bad manners to ask.

Hank, whose right arm was withered from polio, was christened Cordelius Sylvester Price. I was one of the only people who knew Hank's real name because he used his nickname on the sign on his hardware store in the Holler and nobody ever questioned it.

Nicknames were pretty common. I'd be hard pressed to tell you the given names of my buddies: Pig, Sausage, Chew-Chew, and Wormy Whaley. We called the neighborhood Esslinger family the Snot-slingers because it sounded right and poor Carol Stankey, a really cute girl, was nicknamed Stinky because of her last name.

Mrs. Price occasionally slipped and called her son Cordelius, especially if she was in a hurry for some reason. When I asked her about it, she laughed and told me that was his real name.

"So, what do you have for me today?" Mrs. Price asked from her front porch.

"I have some of the biggest, greenest tomatoes you've ever seen, Mrs. Price," I called out as I made my way up her walk. "You can fry some up now and leave the others on a windowsill to ripen up. They are guaranteed to be scrumptious either way!"

Mrs. Price, who seemed older than my mother, always liked my enthusiasm. So much so that in the fall and winter, she gave me a-dime-a-bucket to bring her lump coal in from the coal shed and break it up with a hammer so it would fit in her fireplace. I also disposed of her coal ashes in a metal trash barrel and mowed her tiny yard with a push mower. She also paid me a whole dollar to paint her food pantry.

I fished out the *Times-Picayune* to check the want ads from the wire-mesh trash barrel next to the bench.

"Maybe I'll find something in here."

I tore out the page with delivery services, message boys, and novelty vendors, and put it under my arm.

An old man with a neatly cropped beard, wearing a funny-looking wool-felt hat that I later learned was a beret, pointed me in the right direction.

I made my way to the delivery service. There was a row of bicycles with front baskets parked outside. I was handed an application that required an address and phone number, neither of which I had. The same thing happened at a cleaning service a few blocks farther along.

Around 4 p.m., I grabbed a quick bite at a sidewalk eatery. I still had the want-ads and saw an ad for Novelty Vendors at the 1300 block of St. Charles. Having no idea what a vendor was, I decided to find out. I walked briskly about ten blocks to the address. A red panel truck with Novelty Vendors on the side was parked at the curb.

The warehouse garage door was open and I walked in. In the back corner there were several pushcarts shaped like a hot-dog bun with Lucky Dog painted on the side and smaller yellow ones with hot tamales painted on them. There was a lot of noise and activity with men setting up the carts with food supplies. My stomach growled with the smell of chili and freshly chopped onion wafting in the air.

I walked up to the elevated counter where a busy man with gold-rimmed, half-frames parked part way down his nose, looked up over his glasses. His name-badge said Ralph Dubois. He spoke with a raspy voice, smoked a cigar, was heavy set, and slightly bald.

"Can I help you?"

"I'm looking for work."

"Do you want to go out?" He pointed to a pushcart.

I sure do," I said, adding that I could sell just about anything.

"Okay then, no problem. Fill out this card."

I didn't put an address on the card, but carefully printed my brother Joe's full name, Joe Howard Ford. I wrote down my own social security number that I knew by heart.

I handed Mr. Dubois the card and he told another worker to outfit me with a hot-tamale cart. The carts were rectangular, about five-feet-long, and had a gas lantern on top.

Inside the hinged top was a twenty-gallon metal container with a gas heating element underneath. The cart also had a set of thongs and a supply of paper plates and napkins. Placed in the container were fifty dozen hot tamales that were the size of my index finger, individually wrapped in waxed paper. They sold for forty cents a dozen. Commission was ten cents a dozen. By selling all fifty dozen, I could make five dollars.

After showing me how to operate the light and cart, Mr. Dubois pointed to my route on a map.

"Go out the door and turn left on St. Charles, turn right on Melpomene Street and go all the way to Rampart Street. Your customers will be along that route."

During the Depression before I was born, my siblings sold hot tamales door-to-door in Kentucky and after the family relocated, in Tennessee. Mom made the filling that was wrapped in corn husks. The days of the hot tamale routes were often the subject of family conversation. I wondered what Dad would think about my selling hot tamales in New Orleans.

I wasn't even two blocks from the warehouse on St. Charles Avenue when my first customer walked up. He gave me a dollar bill. But I needed sixty cents in change and only had thirty-five cents in my pocket.

"I don't have enough change for this," I said holding the dollar. "I just started to work. But I can give you thirty-five cents."

"That's okay," the man agreed.

I couldn't believe I made my first profit of twenty-five cents. As I moved up the street, I went into a small news store and got change for that dollar. The experience also taught me that if I said I didn't have the exact change, I might get a larger tip.

With my flair for salesmanship, I sold hot tamales all the way to Rampart Street where I saw loaves of bread for a quarter shaped like torpedoes in a bakery window. I went in and bought one stuffed with roast-beef. The sandwich was called a po-boy. I soaked the edges of the bread in the hot juice from my hot tamales—yum! I topped it off with a Coca-Cola from a vending machine at a gas station.

It was about 9 p.m. when I stopped in front of a tavern where people came out and hungrily bought my hot tamales. By 10 p.m., I'd sold more than half of my supply. By 11:30 p.m. after making my way up and down the block, I'd sold all fifty dozen so I extinguished my lantern. To my amazement, I'd received tips that would equal my commission.

As I pushed my cart back toward St. Charles Avenue, a red panel truck pulled up behind me and tooted its horn. I turned around and it was Mr. Dubois, the manager.

"Where you going?" he asked.

"I'm heading back."

"What?"

"Mr. Dubois, I don't have any more to sell."

"Hey, cut out that mister stuff—everyone calls me Ralph."

Happy to oblige because no matter how hard I tried, I kept mispronouncing Dubois "Duboys" and was tired of being corrected.

I gave Ralph twenty dollars from my sales which he put in a small envelope and wrote my name on it. I kept my tips separate. He opened the door to the back of truck, told me pull my cart around and he would tow it. I sat in the back, holding onto the cart, while we drove to the warehouse.

Once at Novelty Vendors, Ralph put my envelope along with money he collected from the other vendors in the safe. He said it was dangerous for vendors to have a lot of cash on them. Then I helped him load supplies in the truck.

Ralph let me ride with him as he resupplied the hot dog vendors. While we were driving around Ralph offered me a beer, which I declined, but I did accept some cheese that he had.

"Where did you learn to sell like that?"

"My brothers, sisters, and me have sold just about everything around our old neighborhood from tomatoes to soap."

Ralph nodded and I was relieved he didn't ask me any more questions. I needed to keep my story straight about my age and background and didn't want to slip up by revealing too much.

There were about twenty Lucky Dog locations, most in the French Quarter, and Ralph gave me three dollars for helping him. I was amazed with all the bright lights and music and by the sheer number of people out at that time in the morning.

Once we were back at the warehouse, the vendors started returning with their pushcarts. Barbara, a businesslike woman, sitting at a desk behind the counter, added up the sales for each vendor and figured out their commission. She handed me an envelope with five dollars inside. With that, the three dollars from Ralph, my tips and the money I had from Al—I was rich!

It was about 6 a.m. and I was told to return that afternoon if I wanted the work. As I was getting ready to leave, I chatted briefly with the cart maintenance man, who was sweeping up at the warehouse. I asked Merle if he knew of a place where I could stay. He told me to walk down St. Charles and make a left on St. Mary's Street and continue to the corner of Magazine and Camp streets where there was a mission that served as a men's overnight shelter.

I followed the directions and just across from the mission was a café. Although dog-tired and sleepy, I made my way through a plate of huge pancakes slathered in butter and syrup and a cup of coffee for a total of thirty cents. It was the best meal I'd ever had. Then I sat down on a stoop outside, nodding off for a few minutes, and waited for the mission to open. When the doors opened, men started pouring out.

I went inside and saw the sign that beds were fifty cents a night. The clerk, who was about the ugliest, nastiest-looking person I'd ever seen, sat behind a wire security cage.

"You'll have to come back at 6 p.m. because we don't offer beds during the day," he said. There were sweat stains under the arms of his short-sleeve shirt. He clearly had not shaved in a week and most of his front teeth were missing.

It was going to be a challenge to win him over.

"I've been up working all night selling hot tamales and need a place to sleep right now," I said in an assertive but polite manner. "I'm new in town and really need my job. If I don't get some sleep, I won't be able to work tonight."

"Where you from?" he drawled. "Don't sound like you are from N'Orleans."

Thinking he was softening up a bit, I kept the conversation going.

"I traveled here from East Tennessee to get a fresh start and don't have any family to speak of." I wasn't proud of the fib about my folks.

"Tennessee, huh? They're all right." Turns out he had cousins in Chattanooga.

"Okay then," he said and I handed him the fifty cents.

He told me to go up the steps to the second floor and take a bed all the way in the back. I followed his directions. The cots were lined up in rows of ten down one side and up the other and were mostly empty except for a couple of winos still passed out. I found a cot in the back of the room. The sheets were clean, pressed and had a great smell, as if they were laundered with bleach. I was able to get a good five or six hours of sleep. It was the first time I'd been in a real bed since I'd left home.

Waking up from a deep sleep around 2 p.m., I panicked about my money. I jumped up and nervously pulled out my bills. After carefully counting and refolding them, I gave the coins in my pants pocket a reassuring shake.

I washed my face in the restroom using damp paper towels to wipe around my neck and underarms. I headed out to do some exploring around New Orleans before reporting back to work.

Taking in as much of the scenery as I could, I walked up and down the streets and alleyways for a couple of hours. It's hard to describe the freedom I felt. Although still just thirteen, with each step I took, I felt more confident. I stopped at a small eatery where I grabbed another roast beef po-boy sandwich slathered with mustard and onion.

When I bought a Coca-Cola at a filling station, the attendant reminded me of my friend back home in

Happy Holler. Rail worked at the Gulf Station at the corner of N. Central and W. Oklahoma Avenue.

Rail's station had two gas pumps, one high-test and one regular with a gallon of regular selling for about twenty-five cents.

The first time I met Rail, I stopped to get a handful of roasted Spanish peanuts from the peanut machine outside by the door. I inserted a penny and turned the knob but nothing dropped into the slot.

"Having trouble with that gosh-darn machine?" asked Rail, a short, black man in his fifties with a skinny build.

"I put my penny in and nothing came out! I don't have another to spare."

Rail joggled the machine until the peanuts dropped. He then treated me to a five-cent Coca-Cola.

"Now take a swig of the Coke, drop the peanuts into the bottle and sip the Coke chewing the nuts as they reach your mouth."

"Wow, that's neat." I crunched on the soaked peanuts. The combination was tasty with the added bonus of extending the life of the bottle of Coke.

After that Rail and I became good friends. When times were slow, we sat on the curb watching people while he waited for customers. Everybody in the Holler knew Rail, who was congenial, possessing all the social graces with a kind word and friendly wave for passersby. He shared with me his philosophy about work: always treat customers with respect and they will come back again and again.

Rail wore a straw fedora with a silk hatband, church clothes, and brown-and-white two-tone shoes on the KTL bus from the black section of Knoxville to the Holler every day. He changed into blue coveralls, a work cap, and boots at the service station.

With a bulging right eye that didn't line up with his left, Rail had limited vision. After knowing me a while, he let me help him under the rack, wiping the grime off grease fittings so he could see where to aim the pneumatic grease gun to complete the lube job. I never asked Rail about his "bad" eye because I thought it might be a sensitive issue.

<hr />

Once back at Novelty Vendors, Ralph assigned me to a hot-tamale cart. But I already had ambitions of being promoted to the hotdog carts because they paid more and I could work in the French Quarter. Commission on a twenty-five-cent hotdog that was loaded with chili, onion, and mustard was seven cents.

Business was slow on Sunday night when I started. Tips were scarce because most of the bars were closed. Still I managed to sell my hot tamales by around 2:30 a.m. and parked my cart with its lantern extinguished at the same gas station to use the bathroom where I had bought the Coca-Cola the night before.

While I was inside, a big sedan pulling out of the filling station broadsided my cart, knocking it over. The car continued on; there were no crowd and no police around.

"Holy crap!"

Scared I might be fired, I up-righted my cart, which was still functional, and started pushing it back toward the warehouse. Ralph, who collected money from me earlier, soon pulled up behind me, saw the damage, and we towed the cart in. He asked whether I had my lantern lit or not.

"If your lantern had been on, maybe the cart wouldn't have been hit."

"Mr. Dubois...I mean Ralph, I turned it off because I didn't have any hot tamales left and I didn't want people coming up to me. I'm sorry but I thought that was the right way to do it."

"From now on, make sure that light stays on any time after dark until you get back to the warehouse," Ralph said.

At the warehouse while waiting to collect my pay, Merle approached me to see if I was comfortable staying at the mission. I said I wanted a regular place. He told me there was a unit beside his, in a duplex on St. Mary's Street that had been empty for a while and would rent for about twenty-five dollars a month.

"If you can stop by later in the day, I'll introduce you to the property manager," said Merle. "And maybe you can come to some kind of financial arrangement."

After having another breakfast of pancakes and coffee at the café by the mission, I walked around the city for a while before heading over to the duplex where I met up with Merle and the property manager.

The one-room apartment was in a freestanding, light-green stucco building with big front steps. The unit was so tiny that when standing in the middle of my room with my arms extended, I could almost touch the opposite walls at the same time. There was a small sofa with a pull-out bed, a hot plate, sink, toilet, and shower stall.

After some negotiation, the property manager agreed that I could split the first month's rent by paying $12.50

for two weeks with the promise to pay the remaining $12.50 at the end of two weeks. I would then be on schedule with the next payment being twenty-five dollars for the full month.

I paid and took the keys. I immediately went shopping for some incidentals to clean up with like soap, a toothbrush and toothpaste, a towel and also bought some badly needed new underwear. My old briefs were so grungy, I threw them away. Although the stall was moldy, I took my first shower since leaving home and it really felt good. I pulled the sofa bed out and took a nap on the bare, stained mattress.

Waking up about 4 p.m. in my new quarters, I made my way over to Novelty Vendors, grabbing a sandwich on the way. Although my fourteenth birthday was still three months away, I felt like a grownup with a new job, my own pad, and sense of independence.

"Yup, New Orleans is the place. I'm gonna like it here."

Chapter Six

BOURBON STREET

After two nights of peddling hot tamales, I was promoted to hotdog sales when a regular vendor didn't show up. The metal carts were the coolest. They were seven-feet long and looked like a giant hotdog with Lucky Dog painted on the side. They had a grocery-cart handle and stainless-steel-covered steamer heated by an oil stove with separate compartments for the hotdogs, chili, and buns.

It felt like I'd gotten my first set of wheels. As I whistled the Hank Williams tune "Hey Good Lookin'," I ran my hands over the handle and sides of the cart while the lyrics played in my head.

Ralph asked Merle to stock me with a hundred hotdogs that would pay a seven-dollar commission. That night and the next two nights, my route would include

Mary's Tavern, Davy Jones Locker, and the Triangle Bar by Magazine and Camp streets.

The Cajuns hung out on Magazine Street. With their way of talking and my hillbilly accent, we got our point across with hand signals and by repeating simple words.

I relished being a hotdog salesman and took extra care getting the stove going, making my chili, cutting up the onions, putting the buns in the steamer, and fixing up the bottles of ketchup and mustard.

To keep customers coming back, I learned how to make a hotdog with a warm, soft bun. I topped the hot dog with finely chopped onions and chili, boiled down so it was not too thick and not too thin.

I was equipped with thongs, a large spoon for the chili, and a butcher knife for cutting the onions. It was easy to make a loud noise by banging the butcher knife on the metal cart handle and pushing the cart with the other hand as I made my way along a dark street.

On my first night out while pushing my hotdog cart from Mary's Tavern to the Triangle Bar, a drunk with a bottle of cheap Thunderbird wine under his arm came up begging for a hotdog. With an untrimmed beard, long stringy hair, and bad teeth, the poor wino reminded me of the drunks in Happy Holler. His graying eyes had a sad look as he offered me the socks off his feet for a hotdog.

The wino got me thinking about Knoxville and my buddy Roger. There was a silent understanding between us because we both had difficult dads.

While my Dad was a teetotaler and often cruel, Roger's dad Austin England was a sweet man but an alkie. He'd stagger around the neighborhood on his way back from Happy Holler. Often, he'd pass out and fall flat into somebody's yard.

Sometimes I wished my father drank if it could've made him easier to get along with like Roger's.

My Dad's idea of fun was creeping down the basement stairs yelling "water boys, water boys" and throwing a bucket of cold water on David, Joe, and me for the crime of sleeping in past six in the morning.

There was always a racket going on at home with Dad's rages and rivalries among my siblings. Sometimes conflicts erupted into family violence including the evening that my brother Don struck Dad over the head. Dad confronted Don and our sister Mary, who were late getting home from their part-time jobs because they snuck out to the movies. When questioned, they didn't fess up about where they'd been.

Mom took up for them, infuriating Dad. Dad grabbed Mom by her apron in the kitchen and spun her around. As he went into a fury, cursing and becoming more physical, Don grabbed the meat tenderizer mallet and hit Dad over the head from behind.

Dad, with blood streaming down his head, made Don go with him in our old sedan to the hospital where they stitched him up.

As a reminder of his evil deed, Don was forced to sleep with the mallet under his pillow for several nights. Dad pinned his bloody, long-sleeved blue shirt overhead on the trellis in the hallway where it stayed for years.

<hr />

My heart went out to the wino, but I couldn't give him a hotdog because I was answerable for those. I fixed him two buns with chili.

"Here you go," I said.

"Oh my," he said, as his eyes opened wide. "This'll do just fine."

He placed the chili buns and the wine bottle on the sidewalk to remove his worn, unmatched ankle-high boots and pull off his socks. He handed me his socks.

"No thanks, you might need them and I've got some." I lifted my pantleg and pointed.

I watched as the wino put his dirty socks into his pocket and slipped his bare feet back into his unlaced boots. He picked up his chili buns and wine before moseying off.

On my second night, a man dressed as a priest, who was drunk as Cooter Brown, approached me for a hotdog in front of the Triangle Bar. Although there was a Catholic church in North Knoxville, I'd never seen a priest up-close. This priest was so tipsy he had trouble getting his money out. Once he had the hotdog in hand, he said, "God bless you, son." I felt kind of special.

Although it was a rough crowd, I did a brisk business by Mary's Tavern that catered to merchant marines and the men that worked along the banks of the Mississippi River. I even went inside and sold hotdogs to customers sitting at the bar as country music from jukeboxes spilled out into the street.

The night air smelled of beer, bourbon, pee, and sweat.

"Hey, get your chili dogs here! Best hotdogs in New Orleans!" I'd get kidded about the way I said "New Or-LEENZ" instead of "N'OR-lins." The guys at the bar always bought my hotdogs in twos.

When a fight broke out at the Triangle Bar, I was standing just feet away from the door as men were being tossed out onto the street. The bouncers, by sheer physical force, quelled the brawl without the police showing up. For me, it was like watching a fight scene in a movie about the Wild West. When the fight was over, one of the brawlers with a broken nose, busted lip, and bloodied shirt, bought a couple of hotdogs from me.

After three nights, the vendor I was replacing returned to work. Ralph said he had a vacancy in the French Quarter. On my fourth night at Novelty Vendors, I joined the fleet of hotdog carts heading to the Quarter.

Flanked by vendors at least three times my age, I felt like I was part of an army heading into battle to win hungry folks over with a great hotdog. Keeping a tempo, we tapped our butcher knives on the cart handles. Some people applauded or called out as we passed.

I stopped at the corner of Bourbon and St. Peter streets where I set up for the night.

After about two hours, Ralph stopped by to see how I was doing.

"Things are pretty slow, I've only sold five or six hotdogs," I said.

"Don't fret, things will pick up. You'll do well here tonight."

How right he was, the more the people drank, the hungrier they got. After midnight my business really picked up as the crowds grew. Ralph came back around, restocked me, and collected what money I'd taken in.

During my first twelve-hour shift in the Quarter, I had to pee and parked my cart on the sidewalk against the wall near the front entrance at Pat O'Brien's to use the men's room. When I came out, I saw two cab drivers eating hotdogs while standing at the taxi stand across the street. They were laughing. Although they denied it, they stole about a dozen of my hotdogs—big handfuls of them (bare without the buns) and were passing them out.

Two beat cops came around the corner and I pointed excitedly toward the cabbies saying they'd swiped my hot dogs—anywhere from ten to fifteen. One of the cops was as big as a damn mountain.

"Hang on," the big one said to me. The two cops walked up to the cabbies, took no nonsense from them, and collected the money for every single one of the hotdogs, plus some. From then on, I was considered a protected asset in the Quarter and had no problem with any cabbies.

I worked that corner for two nights and was then assigned to Charity Hospital outside the emergency entrance, a tough spot. It was the worst sales night I'd had. I begged Ralph when he came around if he'd get me back to the French Quarter.

The following night I was assigned to the Quarter at the corner of Bienville and Bourbon streets by Arnaud's, the Old Absinthe House, and the Famous Door. If I had to piss at my new location, I waited for Ralph to show up and he watched my cart while I used the bathroom.

The carnival-like atmosphere was like a continuous party with music, lights, and every type of tourist imaginable. Some had foreign accents, but their English was pretty good. They loved American hot dogs and always tipped.

Apart from the hymns my mother played on the piano, country music was all I knew. In the French Quarter, rhythm and blues and jazz flowed freely from the saloons. Musicians like Al Hirt and Pete Fountain were the stars.

I had a flair for casual conversation that kept my regulars coming back. Within a short time, I became known as "Little Joe on Bourbon Street" where I worked seven nights a week. In addition to being a cracker-jack salesman, I'd also become a go-between for customers who would give me a dollar to relay a message such as, "Tell Sammy, I'm at Pat's."

A customer I knew as Lyle would leave a small box to be picked up later by someone else. The first time Lyle left a cigar-size box that felt like it was full of rocks. I later believed it was a test to see if I could be trusted. He gave me five dollars to hold the box. No one came to pick the box up that night so I took it home with me and brought it back the next night. When Lyle, who worked on the docks, returned to pick it up, he could see it hadn't been tampered with and gave me another five dollars.

Lyle had a tattoo on his upper arm of a topless woman in a hula skirt with Aloha written below. He could twitch his bicep to shake the grass skirt. Lyle told me he'd been in the Navy and Hawaii was his favorite place outside of Louisiana.

One time, Lyle left a box that was poorly wrapped and gave me the name of the man who was going to pick it up. Without disturbing the box too much, I carefully peeked inside. It was full of fancy ladies' watches.

Strippers and bartenders in the Quarter were some of my best customers, giving me three dollars for three or four hotdogs and letting me keep the change. I kept all my money in a brown paper bag on top of my shower stall.

When I got home in the mornings, I put my ones and fives in the bag and any change in there too. As the weeks passed, it kept getting fuller and fuller and I thought, "God, I'm getting rich."

I was on a roll. I'd settled into my apartment and bought a new sheet and blanket. I found a laundry a block and a half away. For thirty-five cents, the laundry washed my things and gave them back nicely folded.

At the corner of St. Mary's and St. Charles, stood the Pontchartrain Hotel, which had the grandest, shiniest lobby I'd ever seen. I finally got up the courage to go inside and have lunch at the restaurant. At the hotel I saw a Creole woman, who worked there as a housekeeper. Later, when I was sitting on the stoop in front of my apartment, she was walking home from the hotel and pointed to my unit, asking me if I lived there.

"Yes, this is my place."

"Honey child, do you know there was a man shot in your apartment a few months back? Any idea if he lived or died?"

"What! No one ever told me about that!" I said, scratching my head.

That night at work, I asked Merle about the shooting—thinking he would know, as he lived in the adjacent unit. He wasn't home when it happened but learned from the property manager that the man survived and the shooter was locked up.

My apartment and Merle's were used in the past by prostitutes to service their customers but nothing was said about a shooting. Neighbors and shopkeepers were tight-lipped about the crime.

Could there be a pile of money hidden in my pad and that's why the guy was shot? I'd seen "Night of the Hunter" with Robert Mitchum, the scariest movie ever!

I checked my walls inch by inch for bullet holes and looked for anything that might hold some dough. I tore apart my down pillow, the only thing in my unit that was suspect. A bunch of feathers flew everywhere but no cash.

I settled down but wasn't sure what to think about a near murder occurring in my very apartment. I was glad the guy didn't die or my pad might've been haunted.

Spending money didn't come easily for me —I liked to see it pile up. But I decided I'd better unload some of it so there'd be less for someone to steal. I shopped for some new clothing including another shirt, pair of pants, more socks, and underwear. I also bought a used, brown leather, two-suiter Samsonite suitcase from a second-hand store for six dollars.

I went to Maison Blanche department store where a pair of shiny black dress pants with pink piping down each leg caught my eye. I also found a black t-shirt and a pair of black leather shoes with pointed toes. After trying the outfit on, I paid for it and wore it out of the store. I put my old clothes in a bag and looked like a million bucks strutting home along St. Charles Avenue.

A couple of weeks later, I noticed in the display window of a men's store on Canal Street—a black and pink zip-up jacket for eight dollars. The pink was on the yoke above the breast pockets. I went inside and tried on the jacket that was made of rayon and matched the pants I'd bought at Maison Blanche. I paid for the jacket and decided to save my new clothes for a special occasion.

Before work, I spent time exploring Lafayette Park and walking along the river. I was creepily fascinated by the cemeteries filled with dead people buried in tombs above ground. I stopped in at Café du Monde where I got some "square doughnuts" called beignets with confectionary sugar and coffee for twenty-five cents.

At work, Ralph continued to be impressed with my sales ability and described me as a real enterprising kid.

<hr/>

I'd heard the word "enterprising" before. Two summers ago, I made a deal with the manager of the new Freezo in Happy Holler that featured a walk-up window. It served soft-serve ice cream that none of us kids had ever had. The Freezo didn't have any inside seating, so customers either ate in their cars or sat on the retaining wall on one side of the parking lot.

By closing time, rubbish would be all over the parking area and driveway. The manager said I displayed an enterprising nature when I offered to pick up the trash in exchange for a chocolate-malted. He liked the arrangement and I became a regular helper. If there is something better than a Freezo malt on a hot summer night, I haven't tried it yet.

⋄⋄⋄⋄⋄⋄⋄⋄⋄⋄⋄⋄⋄⋄⋄⋄⋄⋄⋄⋄⋄⋄⋄⋄⋄⋄⋄⋄⋄

As the weeks passed, I continued selling hotdogs at my corner—always disposing of my initial supply of one hundred. After regularly selling close to two hundred, Ralph increased my allotment. I told him I needed to be able to supply customers asking for anywhere from one to ten hotdogs at a time. On average, I was selling 1,000 hotdogs a week. The tips were great and exceeded my commission.

It didn't faze me working on Thanksgiving, Christmas Eve, Christmas, and New Year's because I was so caught up with being a hotdog salesman. It was a life I'd never imagined.

⋄⋄⋄⋄⋄⋄⋄⋄⋄⋄⋄⋄⋄⋄⋄⋄⋄⋄⋄⋄⋄⋄⋄⋄⋄⋄⋄⋄⋄

In truth, holidays with my family were never particularly special. If the day ended without yelling, doors slamming, and someone leaving in a huff—then it was memorable.

At home on Christmas Eve, we hung our socks on the mantel and in the morning, they'd be filled with Horehound candy sticks, a peppermint stick, and maybe an orange. The only toy I ever received on Christmas was a jigsaw puzzle of a ship at sea that I thought was re-gifted to me.

Still, I always counted the gifts for me under the tree on Christmas Eve. I clearly remember one Christmas, when my sister Ethel and her husband Jack arrived unannounced late at night with my two nephews who were much younger than me. I counted four gifts that night but on Christmas morning, two of my gifts had been reassigned to Ethel's sons since there were no gifts for them.

One was a box of chocolate-covered cherries that Tommy wouldn't share. These cherries were the hit of Christmas and I was really jealous because they were intended for me. Bobby got a new pair of socks also meant for me. I was angry, sulked, and stormed out into the neighborhood.

I turned fourteen on January 26, 1956. Although I didn't shave, I'd been successful passing for sixteen and didn't want to press my luck. I was worried if I shared the fact it was my birthday, someone might remark that I looked too young to be turning seventeen.

I enjoyed celebrating alone by devouring an appetizing lunch of red beans and rice at the Pontchartrain Hotel before going to work that night. I was feeling pretty good about myself. With a place to live, a job I loved, and money coming in—I'd planned to stay in New Orleans forever.

But things at Novelty Vendors were changing. Another vendor business was trying to horn in on Novelty's territory, resulting in turf battles.

With the Mardi Gras carnival just around the corner, the rivalry was heating up. One of the Lucky Dog salesmen was run down by a car as he was pushing his cart to the Quarter. The vendor had to be hospitalized and his cart was destroyed.

Following that incident, several vendors reported being yelled at, harassed, and threatened by people they didn't know. Some of the guys were afraid to show up for work.

When I reported to work, I focused on getting my hotdog cart ready but could sense tension in the air at the warehouse. Ralph often went into the office with the owners, shutting the door behind him.

On a chilly Saturday night in early February, I pushed my cart to my corner at Bourbon and Bienville as usual. I set up by putting extra hotdogs in the steamer, stirring my chili and waiting on a couple of customers. The star-filled sky and temperatures in the high fifties were perfect for selling hotdogs.

But around 8:30 p.m. just as my sales were picking up, a black Packard sedan careened down Bourbon Street the wrong way from Canal at a high-speed attempting to make a left onto Bienville.

Luckily, I had my eye on the sedan, which was traveling too fast to make the turn. The sedan kept coming at breakneck speed. I froze in place for a second before my instincts took over. In the nick of time, I leapt out of the way, landing on all fours on the sidewalk as the car nailed my cart to the lamppost between Arnaud's and Stormy's Casino Royale. The impact knocked the lamppost down and crushed my cart against the building. The car missed me by inches as my hotdogs, buns, and chili splattered everywhere.

The driver climbed out of the wreckage and ran back toward Canal Street. I jumped behind the barker, who was standing in front of Stormy's, and followed him into the strip club for safety. I didn't want to be outside when the cops arrived as they might question me.

"You okay?" the barker asked as strippers and patrons flooded toward the door to see what the ruckus was.

"That was a close call!" My hands were shaking.

About five minutes later, I was back out on the sidewalk trying to assess my situation when Ralph showed up in the red truck.

"Are you hurt?" he asked

"No, I'm fine but a little rattled."

We cleaned up whatever we could, leaving the wrecked cart propped against the wall in an alleyway, before driving back to the warehouse in silence. I sensed from his anxious demeanor that this wasn't the time to ask Ralph what the heck happened.

Once at Novelty Vendors, Barbara had my pay envelope ready. She had a no-nonsense manner, smoked using a silver cigarette holder, and drove a white Cadillac.

"Here is your pay," she said, handing me the envelope. "Take it."

Then she demanded, "It's time for you to go back home—and I don't mean to your apartment but wherever you came from."

Barbara stepped out from behind her desk and motioned for me to follow her. We climbed into her Cadillac. She asked me where I lived and quickly drove me the few blocks to my apartment on St. Mary's Street.

"Now, go in and get your things. I'll wait here."

"Yes, Ma'am."

Still reeling from shock of nearly being taken out by the Packard, I didn't try to change her mind.

I grabbed my leather suitcase, quickly threw everything I owned in there, including my pink and black outfit that was still on hangers. I put the paper bag full of money from the top of the shower stall under my arm and went outside.

I put my suitcase in the back seat and Barbara drove me to the bus station on Canal Street. On the short drive, she said that she'd been concerned about me all along. She thought I was too young to be on my own and I was likely a runaway.

"Now you go back home," she said bluntly as she dropped me off.

Chapter Seven

HOME AGAIN

S melling like booze, food, and cigarette smoke, I had on denims and a long-sleeved shirt stained with yellow mustard when I strode into the bus station at ten o'clock. After being yanked out of my job and my pad—I wasn't sure what to do.

Checking out the schedule, I thought, "There's no way I'm going back to Knoxville."

"Brownsville, Texas—now, that's the place." That bus was leaving at 10:35 p.m.

I knew nothing about Texas other than it was the biggest state in the U.S.A. and bordered Mexico, but I loved Westerns on TV. Hopalong Cassidy, who wore a huge black cowboy hat with dimple at the top of the crown, was my favorite.

I walked up to the ticket window and opened my pay envelope.

"Holy crap!" Barbara had put $100 in fives and tens inside. I had to sit down and my hands trembled as I thumbed through the bills twice to be sure I'd counted right. Yup, a hundred bucks! There were ten, crisp fives and five, crisp tens.

"Wow, she really wanted me to go home." I never suspected she'd been looking out for me. I gave the booking clerk fifteen dollars for a Brownsville ticket and got a dollar in change.

Twenty minutes before my bus, I went into the men's room, opened my suitcase, put on my black-and-pink rayon pants and jacket, and black pointed shoes. There was a ding on the floor when the steel barrel key to my apartment fell out of my pants pocket. I picked it up and ran my hands over it before placing it inside the webbing in my suitcase beside my Doyle's ashtray. I combed my hair and repacked, throwing away some well-worn underwear to make room for the paper bag with my money.

Sitting down in the waiting room, I watched people come and go. The sight of a mom and three kids made me think of home. Their belongings were packed into two, five-gallon lard buckets. We used empty lard buckets for storage.

When I heard the announcement for the Memphis and Nashville bus, it got me to thinking. "Shit, what am I gonna do in Texas?"

Homesickness suddenly took hold of me and I went back up to the window. For a couple more dollars I exchanged the Brownsville ticket for the bus to Memphis and Nashville. The timetable showed that travelers could switch buses in Nashville for Knoxville.

The bus was leaving in fifteen minutes so I didn't have time to change my mind again. After checking my suitcase with the driver, I boarded the Memphis bus that had come from Baton Rouge and made my way toward the rear. I sat diagonally across from a woman traveling with her daughter who looked to be about my age. The girl was in the aisle seat.

The girl and I struck up a conversation. "Hi, I'm Loretta and I'm a sophomore," she said, extending her white-gloved hand. I remember thinking she looked like Debbie Reynolds, with big green eyes, curly light brown hair, a turned-up nose, and the sweetest smile.

Apart from my sisters, who could rattle on for hours, she was the chattiest girl I'd ever met. Her mother told us to sit together so she could get some sleep.

I moved over to the window seat and Loretta slid in beside me.

Loretta, who wore a light-blue sweater, plaid skirt, bobby socks, and penny loafers, was quite impressed with my fancy clothes.

"Are you a rock 'n' roll singer?" she asked, batting her eyelashes. "Do you like Elvis Presley?"

Smiling, I let Loretta believe whatever she wanted. Truthfully, I'd only just heard of Elvis having seen an excerpt from his TV debut on a television in the window of an appliance shop in New Orleans.

It was the second time that I thought I might be in love. I had a crush on the young Creole girl who worked at the laundry near my apartment on St. Mary's Street; she flirted with me when I came in. But we only made eyes at each other.

Loretta and her mother were on their way to Cincinnati and had been visiting her grandparents in Louisiana. I told her I was from a big family. Her eyes opened wide when I said I had seven brothers and eight sisters.

When talking about my family, I always included Edith and Junior, who both died as babies. Edith died as an infant long before I was born. My only memory of Junior, who was about eighteen months younger than me, was him sitting in a little chair. His mouth was surrounded with bright orange squash like he'd put up a good fight not to eat it. The second summer of his young life, he took sick and died. By keeping Edith and Junior in my sibling count, I felt like they wouldn't be forgotten.

Loretta and I chatted all the way to Memphis where I treated her to a Coca-Cola at the soda fountain in the bus station.

Loretta kept the conversation going on the next leg of the trip while I listened and nodded my head in agreement to whatever she said. Having never met such a captivating girl, a little shyness came over me.

We talked through the night to Nashville where I planned to change buses to Knoxville and Loretta and her mom would head to Cincinnati. There was enough time for me to buy Loretta breakfast at the snack bar, always within sight of her mother.

When their bus to Cincinnati arrived, Loretta kissed me on the cheek before getting onboard. Although I blushed, I was on top of the world. She waved goodbye from the bus window; I smiled at her and waved back.

During the three-hour bus ride to Knoxville, I spent most of the time staring at the lights out the window, thinking about Loretta, and my life in New Orleans. I would've stayed in New Orleans forever if it hadn't been for that crazy Packard taking out my cart and almost killing me.

I let my thoughts drift to my Dad and got that old, uncomfortable feeling about living with him again. The only good thing about our move to Dry Gap Pike was Dad had to sell our hillside land at Black Oak Ridge where we raised hogs and goats to get the down payment.

⁂

Joe, David, and I were the farmworkers of my generation at Black Oak Ridge. Under Dad's relentless domination, we built two crude, one-bedroom houses with any scrap or used lumber we could get our hands on. At first, the houses had no running water or indoor plumbing and no central heat. Poor people needed affordable places to live. Dad, who was always looking for ways to make a buck, rented the houses for about twenty dollars a month, well below the market rate.

We spent an entire summer using shovels, a pick axe, and wheelbarrows digging out the land to make it level enough for an additional bedroom at the back of one of the houses where Dad could get thirty dollars a month.

We installed an electric jet pump and built a cinderblock pumphouse at the well, so water could be piped to our rentals, along with a tiny country store, a church, and a neighboring house across the gravel road from the farm.

That project involved digging a ditch through hard clay that was as long as a city block to lay the pipe deep enough, so it wouldn't freeze up in the winter. Soon thereafter, Dad started his own informal water company and charged about two dollars a month for running water to the store, church, and neighboring household.

One day we took Lizzie Oates, who'd been living at the adjacent county-owned rock quarry, to Maloneyville, the poor farm east of Knoxville. Lizzie had been living out there for a couple of years in a small canvas tent with only kerosene lamps. We'd look in on her and bring her food and blankets until the day we found her during a rainstorm becoming sickly while sleeping under an umbrella in her leaky tent. Lizzie was no more than five feet tall and couldn't have weighed more than ninety pounds. She was probably in her fifties but looked like she was a hundred. After we loaded her up in our old pickup truck, Joe, David, and I rode in the cargo bed with Lizzie and her meager belongings for the trip.

That same summer when we brothers were helping put a tin roof on the barn at Black Oak Ridge, we disturbed a hornet's nest by pulling out some sheets of tin from a scrap pile encompassed by honeysuckle. We took off trying to outrun the hornets as Dad called to us from the roof.

"You boys get back here!" he yelled, but soon realized why we were on the run. Dad ended up accidentally hitting himself in the head with a hammer while trying to bat the hornets away, causing him to lose his balance and tumble off the roof.

We ran a lot slower to get back to him and pull him up from a patch of musk thistle. He spewed a string of four-letter words that turned my ears red. Normally, we'd be scared shitless had it not been so funny seeing our normally powerful Dad so helpless.

Dad had a few stings, scrapes, and bruises that paled in comparison to his mood—he was literally mad as a hornet. So, we kept any chuckling to ourselves about seeing him in that painful predicament.

<hr/>

It was about 10 a.m. when I walked outside the Knoxville bus station with my suitcase and caught the KTL bus to the bottom of Scott Avenue. I confidently strode up the street to Betty and Glen's house.

My little nephews, Chuckie and Skippy were the first to see me, followed by Glen and then a groggy Betty who had worked the night shift at the telephone company.

Glen, who was known as "Big Foot" in the Holler because of his height and the size of his feet, was cleaning up after fixing breakfast earlier for the family. He heated up some leftover biscuits and fried me a couple of eggs and slices of bacon. I was starved because I hadn't had a bite since Nashville.

"Connie, so where've you been?" asked Glen. "Your father and David drove around for weeks looking for you." Glen was my Dad's favorite son-in-law. Dad always said he was plain spoken and honest as the day is long.

Glen and Betty, whose eyes drifted back and forth to my fancy clothes, said the family thought for sure I'd been kidnapped and likely killed.

While sharing some details about my trip and my job selling hotdogs in New Orleans, I tried to act concerned about causing people to worry. But, truthfully, it hadn't occurred to me that my family might be upset I was gone. I found it kind of nice they were.

In the midst of my story, Betty called Mom and Dad and said she and Glen would take me home. The ride took less than thirty minutes. Going up our driveway gave me a weird feeling, as if I was going back in time. The months away suddenly seemed like they'd gone by in an instant.

"Are you going to stay for a while?" That was the only thing my Dad said as I walked inside.

"Yup, plan to."

There were no hugs, no kisses. Mom had tears in her eyes so I knew she was glad to see me.

We sat down and I shared my story about hitchhiking all the way to New Orleans and about selling hotdogs in the French Quarter. Dad shook his head in disbelief.

I thought it best to leave out the part about cashing the bad checks in Florida. When Annie commented on my spiffy clothes and shoes, I told her they were latest style in New Orleans.

Then before I knew it, I was unpacking my suitcase on my bed in the enclosed back porch that I shared with David and Bill. Keeping it as a memento, I put my apartment key in a little slit on the side of my mattress along with my Doyle's ashtray.

I changed into my regular clothes and shoes, folding my New Orleans duds and placing them into my suitcase for safekeeping. I gave my mother nearly all the cash I'd saved up. Along with Barbara's new bills and my wrinkled, sweaty ones, it amounted to about $300. I kept just a few dollars for myself.

Mom was always hiding things so I suspect she put the money into the baking powder tin on top of the kitchen cabinet.

"Connie, I'll put this away for you if you ever need it," she said.

"Go ahead and spend it," I said proudly, knowing I would never see the money again. It didn't bother me at all. I felt good being able to give Mom something that might help a lot.

I went back to school that Wednesday. At first it was strange seeing my classmates. There were stares but not glares. Most kids hadn't been farther away than Knoxville or Nashville and I was a world traveler. I'd grown a little taller and my voice was a little deeper—physical attributes that matched my new self-confidence.

I still had about three months of the eighth-grade left and finished the school year without incident. During my absence, the seventh and eighth grade moved over into a new addition at the high school where Annie was a sophomore and David was a senior.

An eighth-grade friend introduced me to Cliff Sowder, who owned a dairy farm on Old Andersonville Pike. Cliff let me work there two or three afternoons a week cleaning out barn stalls, repairing fencing, and feeding livestock. I walked the two miles to his farm afterschool and hitchhiked home.

Once school was out, I worked for Cliff and several other local farmers pitching hay and storing silage. That was in addition to chores at home. Dad didn't object to me working elsewhere as long as I was getting paid and bringing money in.

Along Dry Gap Pike, I was obsessed with the big-leafed kudzu vines that crawled all over everything in sight, strangling trees, fences, utility poles and wires.

We called them "mile a minute vines" because they grew a foot a day. If I let my thoughts wander, I found their quick growth suffocating as if I was trapped in a horror movie. They gave me nightmares. It didn't help when I was grubbing the vines away from a fencepost with a hoe, I uncovered a den of black snakes that swirled underneath and around my feet, scaring the living shit out of me.

To make matters worse, my troublesome hernia that I got after rupturing myself last fall before I ran off was still a secret and continued to bother me.

One of my chores when we moved to Dry Gap Pike was to slop the hogs before catching the school bus. I had to dip a two-gallon bucket into the fifty-five-gallon feed barrel, drawing the mix of bran, water, and food scraps.

The day I hurt myself, I'd lifted the first bucketful with outstretched arms to prevent any slop from splattering my school clothes. Before emptying it into the hog trough, something pulled in my groin.

The pain was so severe after I returned to the feed barrel for another bucketful, I could barely empty it. It was a burning ache like nothing I'd experienced. My shriek caused the two hogs to look up and grunt.

"Wha'cha lookin' at, you fat asses?"

At that moment, I hated the hogs and hated my life at Dry Gap Pike. If we were still on Scott Avenue, I wouldn't have been in this situation.

Buckling over and hardly able to walk the fifty yards back to the house, I told Mom I was sick. But after lying down for a few minutes, I got to feeling better and went on to school.

I didn't tell my parents because it was an issue in my private area. Whenever my injury bothered me, I'd lie down, push the bulge in my ball-sack up with my fingers, and the swelling would go away.

I looked up hernia in the encyclopedia in the school library. My visits to the library had been non-existent, so I was careful not to alert the librarian about what I was researching. I read that some people would wear a device

called a truss that held their insides up when they had
my problem.

The hernia's presence was never far from my mind,
but I tried to go on as if nothing had happened.

One thing I noticed on my return to Dry Gap Pike
was, with fresh air and exercise, Bill seemed happier in
the country. I could see why Dad wanted to move him
from the city. For hours on end, Bill loved riding his small
Farmall tractor, pulling an old cultivator disk around and
around in the large open field behind the house.

While I loved the old Bill, before he was sick, I was
ashamed of the new Bill. When we still lived on Scott
Avenue in the city, I worried that Bill would be labeled
as cuckoo having been wary of two of our neighborhood
characters, "Crazy Bill" and "Sarg."

Crazy Bill lived a few doors up, was in his forties,
and had parents older than mine. He had closely cropped
graying hair and was very short in stature. Crazy Bill was
always clean-looking in a plain, long-sleeved shirt and
dress pants. He also wore old black leather shoes that
turned up at the toe. Crazy Bill always gave me a beady-
eyed look when I passed by so I walked on the other side
of the street if he was out.

Unable to tolerate the arrival of a single leaf or any dirt, Crazy Bill constantly swept the sidewalk and front walkway to his house with an old broom. Windy days upset him. One day he got very frustrated, left his yard, and went down East Scott Avenue toward the Holler with the broom in hand. The police were called to help find him and take him home.

Although our Bill was nothing like Crazy Bill—I worried my brother would be labeled like that.

Another odd fellow was World War I veteran Sarg, who was balding and had a muscular build. He spoke with an abnormally loud voice. He was proud of his pocketknife and had a distinct dislike for all kids, telling us to "get outta here!" whenever we approached.

Sarg, who lived alone, threatened to cut my ear off if I came near his buckeye tree.

~~~~~~~~~~~~~~~~~~~~~~~~~~~~~~~~

Despite being in the country, Bill still didn't like loud noises. He startled easily and didn't want to be hollered at. He was upset when motorists—who were only trying to say hello—blew their horn and waved when he was working in the front yard. Muttering, he retreated back into the house.

When David and I were doing our chores, we were frustrated with Bill for not helping. One day our resentment boiled over.

"How come we're doing all the work and Bill is still in bed?" I asked.

"Hell, I've had enough—I am going to get Bill up." David went inside and tried to drag Bill out of bed by his ankles.

The next thing I heard was David crying out with a string of cuss words. Bill woke up with a start and popped David in the face giving him a black eye.

Chapter Eight

CINCINNATI

Football was king at my high school. There were pep rallies with the school band, cheerleaders, and adoring fans. I loved it all.

I'd snuck around and played pickup basketball when we lived in Knoxville. I also threw an old football here and there with my buddies. But making the Varsity as a tall, skinny ninth-grader was my first experience with organized sports.

With grass stains and dirt on my uniform, I felt like a warrior walking off the field after practice. Girls smiled at me and the other players. Football was the glue keeping school together for me.

Luckily my hernia wasn't conspicuous when I showered with the team. If the coach knew, I wouldn't be able to play football. But the hernia was the least of my problems.

At Monday practice after our first game on Friday night, Dad and David showed up by the gym just as I was coming out in my practice uniform.

My heart sank when I saw them sitting in the old red pickup truck. Dad had Mondays off work. This couldn't be good. I walked over and stood about three feet away from Dad.

"You don't have time to play football." Dad's dark eyes narrowed. "Get your crap. You're coming home."

I returned to the locker room and kicked the door to my locker, denting it so it wouldn't close. After changing into my school clothes, I squeezed into the front seat beside David. In my head I knew, I should've seen this coming.

Dad became suspicious the week before when he took a sick day and was home when I got there. I told him I'd missed the bus and had to walk. Knowing I was lying because I would've hitched, he made me count the steps between Halls High and our house. He told me report back the next day. I had to miss practice to complete the three-and-a-half-mile task on foot.

As Coach was leaving the gym, he saw me. He walked up to the passenger window.

"My son has work to do. He doesn't have time for this shit." Dad bent toward the steering wheel so he could look eye-to-eye.

Coach didn't try to change Dad's mind about the benefits of sports. Work was a word that teens in Halls Crossroads understood. He'd run into this before.

"Okay. See you around, Conley." Coach slapped the side of the door twice before walking to the field. I took that as a sign he felt bad for me.

Staring out the window, I was too dejected to say a word. If I opened my mouth, I couldn't be responsible for what might spill out. Dad's regular speech about how nobody who played sports amounted to a goddamn thing would be too much to handle.

At home, I confronted David.

"When I got home from school, Dad asked where you were," David said with a wry smile. "I told him you had football practice."

I threatened David with my fist but held back. Punching David would make matters worse. We avoided each other for the rest of the day.

That night with my head buried in my pillow, I yelled "son of a bitch and shit!" over and over.

From the get-go, I'd struggled academically at school. Whether it was Algebra, history, or English—I couldn't focus on academics and didn't do an ounce of homework. There was no support at home for book-learning. Dad believed teachers were paid to teach during school hours. Homework was an excuse to get out of chores.

The rest of the school week, I was like a Zombie. I went through the motions. Even my teammates stayed out of my way.

On Saturday morning after missing our first away game the night before, I fully intended to work at Cliff Sowder's farm. While hitchhiking there, I changed my mind.

The independence I'd enjoyed in New Orleans made me smile. I stopped in at Dozier's country store at the corner of Old Andersonville Pike and Maynardville Pike. Flat broke, I decided to ask Mr. Dozier for a loan.

<hr>

While long afternoons and weekends slogging away at Black Oak Ridge before our move to Dry Gap Pike were over, it didn't change things. With fewer kids at home, less money was coming in. We could barely afford Dry Gap Pike. The backbreaking work making our new place livable, made toiling at Black Oak Ridge seem easy.

Our single-story clapboard house with large front porch had an outhouse, no indoor plumbing, and no central heat. It was a big downgrade from our home on Scott Avenue.

After relocating and widening the driveway, creating additional parking for us and the one-room church next door, we installed a septic system. We converted a small bedroom into a bathroom with shower, sink, and toilet.

We contracted for a new well to be dug and installed an electric pump supplying water to the house. We kept the outhouse as a backup toilet.

We scooped out a stock pond for our animals, fenced five acres, and planted a two-acre garden where we grew potatoes, okra, corn, lettuce, cabbage, tomatoes, peppers, and cucumbers. Raising hogs, chickens, along with a Hereford steer and milk cow, we were mostly self-sufficient for food.

David, Bill, and I slept on the enclosed porch on the back of the house. On really cold nights David and I camped out in the kitchen. Bill just put on more covers. Our parents and sister Annie had the two bedrooms.

When it was bitterly cold, I stood behind the wood-burning stove in the living room to dress. One morning I got too close and burnt a hole in the seat of my favorite trousers. My backside was fine but I was furious about ruining the blue wool pants that had been part of Bill's Air Force uniform and fit me perfectly.

Mr. Dozier's son "H.M." had been a classmate of mine at the Oakwood grade school in Knoxville. They lived in my old neighborhood.

"Mr. Dozier, I'm on my way to Sowder's. He can't pay me till next week. Could you loan me three dollars to get me through?"

During the summer when I worked at Cliff's farm, I often had lunch at Dozier's. Mr. Dozier would fix me a bologna and cheese sandwich.

Mr. Dozier readily agreed to lend me the money and didn't ask why I needed it. He opened the cash register and pulled out three one's.

"Conley, you're a hard worker. Keep it up and you'll go far in life."

I didn't need that kind of encouragement right then. It was hard for me to see the future.

With the three dollars in my pocket, I didn't head to the farm but walked across the road. I hitched a ride going north. Chicago was my final destination.

I hitched a series of short rides from Halls Crossroads to Maynardville to Tazwell, then through the Cumberland Gap, and caught another ride to Middlesboro, Kentucky.

In Middlesboro, a driver in a pickup truck towing a race car on a flatbed trailer stopped. When I got in, I asked if he'd ever raced at the Broadway Speedway, the dirt track in Halls.

"Nope, but it'd be great to race there. I started out on dirt. By the way, I'm Pete Toth."

"Sorry, I didn't recognize you right away. Everyone knows Pete Toth!" Race-car drivers were up there with professional football players in my eyes.

Pete was heading home to Lima, Ohio. He told me he was happy to have me along. He was dog-tired and my company would keep him awake. He gave me a ride all the way to Cincinnati.

Around 7 a.m. Sunday, he dropped me off at the Greyhound station where I said I'd catch the bus to Chicago. I sat down in a chair in the waiting room to take a nap.

After a couple of hours, I woke up and got something to eat at a little cafe. The shops were closed. So, I walked all over the place and kept thinking Cincinnati can't compare to New Orleans or Miami. I grabbed a cinnamon bun at the same café before making my way back to the bus station.

I found a discarded newspaper, dated Nov. 11, 1956, and fell sound asleep face down in the paper. It must have been around eight o'clock when a tap on the shoulder woke me up. My eyes opened to see a uniformed police officer staring at me. He wasn't smiling.

"Are you from Cincinnati?" he asked.

"No, sir."

"Where you headed?"

"Chicago."

"Let's see your ticket, son."

"Don't got one."

"Got any money?"

"A few bucks."

"Come with me," he said. The officer radioed for a police car that arrived in a matter of minutes and took me to the juvenile detention hall. I was so tired that it took me a few minutes to grasp my situation. But riding in a police car sure wasn't all it was cracked up to be.

Inside the juvenile center, I was interviewed by a stony-faced older man in bifocals and a wrinkled suit.

He said I was accused of vagrancy, a word that was new to me. I told him my real name. I said while I had no ticket and no money to speak of, I was on my way to my sister's home in Chicago. He wrote it all down. I think he believed me.

"Can I go now?"

"No, Ford. You'll have to stay here tonight."

He told me to empty my pockets. I put thirty-five cents in change, the dollar bill I had left, and my comb into a large manila envelope.

A young man in a khaki uniform took me upstairs and gave an orange jumpsuit and a towel. He showed me the shower room and told me to clean up. I put my clothes into a cloth bag that was provided.

The same man walked me down the hall and into a large room with no windows and no beds. A huge black man in a blue uniform with his arms folded across his chest sat in a wooden chair in the middle of the room. A bright, ceiling light made a circle around him. He didn't say a word because he didn't have to. His gaze and silence were unnerving.

There were roughly fifteen teenage boys in the room, a mix of blacks and whites. Most were mean-looking and tough as nails. All of us had been picked up the same day for a range of infractions and hadn't been assigned rooms. We were given pillows and blankets.

Tired and scared, I fell asleep hugging my pillow on the floor with my back against the wall. I tried to dream about Florida, oranges, and white sand but couldn't get those thoughts to stick.

In the morning, we were marched down to the cafeteria and stood in line for our food. I purposely didn't make any conversation with the other boys. I wasn't a fighter and was still trying to assess what my next move would be. Was I tough looking? No one ever said I was.

I didn't hear any southern accents so I kept my mouth shut. Growing up, I'd heard plenty about Yankees who looked down on southerners, especially hillbillies. I didn't want to draw any attention to myself.

After we ate, I was taken to an office where the social worker, a friendly-looking woman with a warm smile, asked me who to call. I gave her my sister Betty's phone number. I could hear the woman's half of the conversation.

It was a Monday holiday because Veterans Day fell on Sunday, the day before.

Betty and Glen were both off work. They left their sons with our sister Nona, who was staying with them. They drove six to seven hours from Knoxville to Cincinnati.

They signed some paperwork at the detention center and I was free to go.

On the long drive home, there was not much back 'n' forth conversation. Glen just shook his head while Betty conversed continuously without expecting anyone to chime in. She loved to chat about the switchboard at the telephone company and shared some of the stories she overheard while connecting callers. She'd laugh and say "I don't listen in" and then show me her crossed fingers. Between my naps, her chatter made the time pass quickly.

Once back in Knoxville, I spent the night at Betty's. The next day, with my nephews Chuckie and Skippy along for the ride, she and Glen drove me to Dry Gap Pike.

Dad didn't seem that bothered about my latest brush with the law. He might've been distracted because things at work were really tough for him.

Diesel engines were taking over so the railroad didn't need as many men on a crew. This upset the union that required a man be put on whether there was a job for him or not. Men without jobs reported to work, signed in, and went back home. The railroad company stopped this and the union went on strike.

Dad refused to honor the strike and continued working. The union harassed him by filling the back seat of his car with empty whiskey bottles and sugared his gasoline tank—wrecking the engine.

A week after I got back, Dad presented me with an L&N employee railroad pass to Chicago.

"Connie, if you have a hankering to leave again, use this pass and take the train."

The pass was on a small piece of yellow cardboard, had the date 1956-1957, had L&N Railroad at the top in black lettering. The typing just below that said: Lee J. Ford family pass. I liked the looks of it.

Was Dad concerned about my welfare or hoping I'd go away again? He needed my help with chores, so I didn't dwell on this question.

"Thanks, Dad. This is cool."

"Stay off the roads, Connie. Keep the law off your back."

I dug out my hand-me-down, tri-fold leather wallet. I put the pass inside next to my social security card.

Dry Gap Pike was on the school district border of Halls Crossroads and the unincorporated village of Powell. I transferred to Powell High School for a fresh start.

The day I enrolled, Principal Morris called me into his office to welcome me to his school. It was kind of nice. The last time I was called to the principal, two detectives were waiting for me.

My second week at Powell, I skipped school and hitched to the Roxy Movie Theatre off Market Street in Knoxville to see a double feature. I managed to hitch back home by the time school was out.

I forged an absence note using my best penmanship and brought it to the principal's office the next morning. Mr. Morris handled two or three students with excuses for absences at the same time.

On this particular day, he focused on me and a sophomore named Johnny, whose excuse was more creative than mine.

"Johnny, from the looks of your note, I see you went to the dentist again."

"Yes sir, Mr. Morris, I did."

"Johnny, I have enough notes in my desk from last year to prove you don't have a tooth in your head. Now you both get out of here and go to class."

At Powell there was an area in a narrow courtyard between two buildings where we were allowed to smoke.

I hadn't smoked at all in New Orleans but picked up the habit again because all the cool guys smoked.

I never lit up a cigarette in front of Dad. One of his favorite sayings was "smoking limits a person's ability by one-third."

He said a smoker spends the ten minutes before thinking about a cigarette, then ten minutes smoking a cigarette, and the ten minutes after in the fog of addiction.

My friends and I were experts at bumming cigarettes, a practice we dubbed "OP's" for "other people's." Cigarettes were expensive, about twenty-five cents a pack: Camels and Lucky Strikes were popular. But the cheap brand, Wings, was my favorite.

But mostly, we used Stud Smoking Tobacco that came in a small cloth bag with a drawstring and rolling papers for about ten cents and rolled our own cigarettes.

<hr />

Despite the friendly principal and convenient smoking area, I didn't last at Powell High.

At the start of my fourth week, I left for school that morning but never made it. I can't really explain it. But school wasn't for me. The football season was ending, so there was no chance I could play. Although the kids accepted me, I still felt like the new kid.

I hitchhiked down Emory Road from Powell High to L&N Depot in Knoxville.

At the depot, I showed my pass, got the schedule, and bought some peanuts, a Snickers bar, and a Coke from the vending machines. After milling around Knoxville for a couple of hours, I caught the late-afternoon train to Chicago. I had the clothes on my back, about a dollar in change and told no one I was leaving.

I slept most of the sixteen hours on the near-empty train. I only had enough money for a candy bar. Being hungry, the easiest way to pass the time was to nap. Chicago seemed like the perfect destination because my siblings Don, Joe, and Ethel all lived in the area.

When we stopped in Nashville, I stretched and woke up long enough to watch a black family on the platform get into the segregated rail car. The mother reminded me of Clara who lived across the street from us on Scott Avenue in a tiny bungalow behind the Pinkston house with her husband, Governor. He worked as a sweeper for the railroad. They were the only blacks who lived on our street.

Clara served as the nursemaid for my playmate Nancy Pinkston as well as doing the cooking and cleaning for the family. All the neighborhood kids knew Clara who kept an eye on us and would follow up a scolding with a peanut butter and jelly sandwich.

As I sat there looking out the window, I thought I didn't really get why we had to live in separate neighborhoods and ride in separate rail cars. White or black, we were human beings, trying to survive.

Then I thought about the time when I was around five or six. I was going to Knoxville with Mom on a nearly-empty bus. Two young black boys a little older than me got on at a stop. They sat right down behind the driver. He reached around and grabbed one of them by the knee and said, "You two sit all the way in the back." He wouldn't pull out until they were seated.

I got up to move back with the other boys. Mom yanked me down by the arm and said, "You sit here with me!"

<hr />

After those reflections, I curled up and slept for the remainder of the train ride.

When I stepped onto the platform at Union Station in downtown Chicago and walked to the lobby, I was amazed by the size of the place. I immediately bumped into an old lady with a cane because I was looking all around and not paying attention. She was only slightly jolted and I said, "Pardon me, ma'am."

Once in the lobby, I quickly fixated on the dozens of foreign-looking people lined up in the great hall with big tickets around their necks. Most were young men but there were also some families with small children.

The men were wearing wool hats and the women had scarfs wrapped around their heads. Most were wearing long dark coats and carrying their belongings in cloth bags. From the looks on their faces, I guessed they were scared of something.

I had my brother Don's work number and spent a dime at a payphone to call him. Don worked for Milwaukee Railroad and his office was in Union Station. It only took him about five minutes to find me. He bought me a bite at an eatery in the station. I was starved and wolfed down a juicy cheeseburger and fries.

"What are you doing up here, Connie?" he asked, looking surprised to see me but not shocked.

"I thought I'd come north because you, Ethel, and Joe are up here," I said. "I want to look for work."

Don nodded his head. After all, he grew up the same way I did—looking for a way out. He lived in a rooming house so I couldn't stay there.

While we were talking, he told me the foreigners at Union Station were Hungarians being resettled in the Chicago area. I'd never heard of Hungary but did know about the Soviet Union. Don said they'd squashed a revolt causing a refugee crisis.

Don, who had Mom's sweet disposition, left home when he enlisted in the Army. I hadn't seen him in about three years. He looked like I remembered with sandy-colored hair and hazel eyes. I was a lot taller.

Our conversation included Dad, who believed in corporal punishment but practiced it rarely—preferring other forms of discipline. In fact, I only remember getting a drubbing a couple of times.

Dad said whipping us wasn't effective, as it was over too fast and didn't have lasting effects. As my sisters can attest, his tongue-lashings coupled with loading us down with more chores stung more than any belt ever could.

We talked about the day our sister Nona had been waxing our floors on Scott Avenue. She didn't respond to Dad's call to help Mom outside. Dad took a bag of lime from the chicken coop and spread it all over the newly waxed floors. Nona had to clean it up.

Leaving for the Army before we moved, Don had never been to Dry Gap Pike. He asked if I'd seen his twin Dana, whom he worried about. Dana, who was the sweetest of all our sisters, was living in Georgia and didn't come home often because Dad couldn't stand her husband, John Paul Jones.

Don and I both remembered the day Dana, who at seventeen and had not finished high school, eloped with the love-of-her-young-life John Paul. They got married in the back of a barbershop in Ringgold, Georgia.

On the way to school that morning Dana met up with John Paul and drove the 115 miles to Ringgold, which is just across the state line from Chattanooga. Tennessee required blood tests so getting married would've taken a few days. Dana was in a hurry.

A few days before she left, she was taking a bath and tying up the bathroom too long. She ignored Dad's pleas to hurry up. He peed through the keyhole and she had to clean it up.

Don and I agreed we couldn't blame Dana for leaving any way she could.

After lunch, Don called Ethel, gave me five dollars, and bought me a ticket on the Illinois Central Railroad to Harvey where Ethel lived. He walked me to the right gate.

Chapter Nine

HARVEY

On the forty-five-minute train ride, I stared out the window watching the gray-colored buildings pass by. Chimneys filled the overcast sky with smoke. The bare trees added to the starkness.

"What do people see in being up North?" I wondered. "It sure wasn't the scenery."

Three of my siblings were drawn here by work, so I guessed that was the attraction.

I hadn't seen my eldest sister Ethel for ages but figured she hadn't changed much. She had Mom's light brown hair and square build.

But there was a steely, no-nonsense toughness in Ethel that was more like our father—gained from her girlhood spent helping to raise the younger ones.

My siblings could always picture Ethel, as a young girl, bent over the stove with a wooden spoon in one hand while juggling a baby brother or sister balanced on the opposite hip.

It was midafternoon and freezing when I got to Harvey. With no suitcase, no winter coat and only a light jacket, I buried my hands in my pockets and hunched my shoulders as I walked outside. Light sleet felt like little pin pricks pelting my forehead. To keep from slipping, I gingerly climbed down the steps to the street and got directions to Ethel's address from a passerby.

As I walked along whistling the Marty Robbins's tune "Singing the Blues," it's hard to explain—while I was alone—I wasn't lonely. The catchy country beat suited my mood but not the lyrics. I wasn't blue. I was on the move again, on another adventure, and it suited me.

I often thought that if reincarnation was real then I'd been a cowboy in a previous life. Westerns on TV and in the movies were my absolute favorites. The vast openness and the freedom of the plains appealed to my imagination. I definitely would've gone west during the Gold Rush.

As I passed by a pizza place a short distance from the train station, I stopped for a minute to look in the window. A cook in a white chef's hat was tossing the pizza dough in the air—a feat I'd never seen.

I continued on and wended my way the five blocks from the train station to Ethel's.

There was an empty parking lot next to an old clapboard house that had been converted into apartments. It was around 3:30 p.m. when I went up the front walk with my shoes sliding on the icy pavement. I pounded on the door, despite not being one hundred percent sure I had the right address.

Ethel, who had just come home from her cleaning job at General Felt, answered the door. She did her best to be happy to see me. A call from Don earlier that afternoon was the only notice she had of my arrival.

"Connie, come in—you must be freezing!" She reached for a welcoming hug.

I felt a little strange at her expression of warmth because we Fords were not huggers. But I sighed with relief that I'd found her place without difficulty.

With eighteen years difference in our ages, Ethel and I'd never been close. Yet being part of the same big family created a bond that couldn't be denied by age or distance.

Ethel's ground-floor apartment was too small even for her family, never mind adding a kid brother. As I looked around, my nephews Bobby and Tommy, who were nine and six years old, were playing the Lone Ranger and Tonto. They ran rings around me in the small living room. Ethel's husband Jack wasn't home.

"Connie, why'd you leave home?" Ethel asked.

"I just can't stay there anymore. You know what it's like," I said lighting a smoke. "School, Dad and I don't get along."

Having barely completed the eighth grade, Ethel— pointing to the worn green sofa that would be my bed—nodded sympathetically. While Ethel was a strong woman, there was an undeniable sadness in her eyes.

When she was a teenager, Ethel became pregnant by her boyfriend Ed Monday and nine months later gave birth to Danny. I don't know if Ethel and Ed ever married. Still in diapers myself, I was too young to be aware of any family dynamics. But I did know that Ed wasn't around and only she and Danny lived with us.

Danny and our youngest brother Junior are buried side by side at Lynhurst Cemetery on North Broadway in Knoxville. When the boys died, Dad purchased a family plot in an undeveloped part of the cemetery.

In a quiet moment, Ethel shared with me the guilt she carried—in that, if she'd been able to give Danny up for adoption—he might be alive today. She believed the two babies didn't receive medical care soon enough to prevent the diarrhea and dehydration that killed them. They died during the hot summer in 1944.

A few years after Danny died, Ethel met Jack Patton while working at the nuclear facilities at Oak Ridge. They fell in love, married, and moved to Fayetteville, Tennessee where both their sons were born. When they were laid off at the cotton mill in Fayetteville, they moved to the Chicago area where Jack had a brother and there was plenty of work.

Quiet by nature, sandy-haired, cleanshaven, and handsome with a bright smile, Jack never touched alcohol during the work week. But on weekends, drink transformed him from a reserved, well-mannered man into someone who was full of fun.

From observations in Happy Holler and New Orleans, I knew some alcoholics were mean drunks but not Jack. After a few drinks, he'd become a jokester, picking up the tab at local bars. While his drunken antics made his fellow barflies happy, they made life miserable for Ethel.

Ethel made arrangements with Acme Steel where Jack worked to pick up his wages on Friday afternoons so he didn't spend his entire paycheck before he got home. Ethel would stop at the bank to cash his check, do the grocery shopping, and buy Jack two bottles of whiskey to keep him out of the bars. Like clockwork by 10 p.m. Friday, Jack would have finished the bottle, be in his funny mood and would want to go out. Ethel, who hid the other bottle until the next day, wrestled him to keep him home.

When Jack came home the day I arrived, he pulled out a bottle of Jack Daniel's from the kitchen cabinet. It was a couple of weeks before Christmas and there was some leftover chocolate cake from a birthday celebration for Jack from the day before. Ethel saw me look longingly at the cake and fixed me a slice. Jack helped himself, gobbling a piece down with a shot of straight whiskey.

A year after Ethel and Jack moved to Chicago, our brother Joe and his wife Mary, as newlyweds, moved to Harvey where Ethel helped Joe get a job as a machine operator in the factory at General Felt. Joe had since changed jobs and was working at a grocery store in nearby South Holland.

That Monday after they got home from work, Jack and Ethel, who never learned to drive, and the kids took me shopping for a winter coat, shirt, pair of pants, and underwear at a department store in Chicago Heights. I was impressed with Jack's brand-new light blue 1956 Ford sedan. Ethel complained about the payments they were making on the car. I got the hint. I had to support myself and not add to my sister's troubles.

When Tuesday rolled around, I landed a job as a stock boy at Kroger's grocery store in downtown Harvey, stamping prices with a marking kit on canned goods. I learned how to cut the top of the box off and stamp the top row of cans, put the top back on, flip the box over and stamp the rest. I was working full-time for seventy-five cents an hour.

On my third day, a tractor-trailer showed up with more canned goods and supplies for the store. I helped unload the truck by setting up a conveyor line into the stockroom.

After I'd marked all the cans, the manager saw me restocking shelves using just one hand.

"What's wrong with the other hand?"

Then he showed me how to use both hands, getting the task completed in half the time.

On my first Saturday, the manager asked me if I ever took a fifteen-minute break, a union requirement, and told me to do so. That afternoon I walked across the street to the corner restaurant. I ordered a Coca-Cola. As I sat at the counter, the Kroger manager, who was getting ready to leave, gave me a nod and paid for my soda. That told me he thought I was a good worker.

After my first week with money coming in, Ethel told me about a rooming house the next street over where she knew the landlady. I could rent a room there for ten dollars a week. I wasn't upset that Ethel wanted me to move out. I knew my sleeping on her green sofa was only temporary. I was grateful she helped me find a pad.

I found the old house, met the landlady, who lived on the first floor, and rented a room upstairs. The landlady had a scratchy, hoarse voice as though she smoked and yelled too much.

While inspecting my tiny room that included a single bed and small dresser but had no window, I noticed that both of the door hinges were repaired with leather straps. The lock appeared to have been tampered with. The walls were paper thin. I could hear talking and radios from the other tenants' rooms. I doubted my small, musty room was intended to be a bedroom and had likely been a storage closet.

I bought an electric alarm clock that went missing from my room the very next day. I'd plugged the alarm clock into the only outlet and had to stretch the cord over the bed to put the clock on the dresser. When I asked the landlady about my missing clock, she told me she confiscated it when checking my room because it used too much electricity.

I went out and bought a Baby Ben wind-up alarm clock that made a loud ticking noise. It forced me to put the pillow over my head to muffle the noise until I fell asleep. In the morning, I cussed out loud when I stubbed my toe on the foot of the bed as I jumped up trying to silence the alarm. I then limped to the shared bathroom to clean up for the day and wrapped some toilet paper tightly around my bloody big toe before putting on my socks and shoes.

After a few weeks at Kroger's, the manager called me into the office and gave me unwelcome news.

"Conley, you are a good worker but the union has denied your application due to your age. Legally, you can only work part-time."

I didn't understand what the union had against young workers. I was passing for sixteen, which was old enough to quit school. But, nevertheless, the store cut back my hours.

"Okay then. If it's all right with you, I'll work mornings," I told the manager.

I got a second job afternoons and evenings pumping gas for eighty-five cents an hour at the Road Chief filling station. When I picked up additional work at the station, I gave up my job at Kroger's.

There was a sense of excitement at the Road Chief reminiscent of Happy Holler and I really liked it there.

On one night a platinum blonde woman pulled up in a brand-new, black Lincoln Continental Mark II to get gas. She looked enough like Marilyn Monroe to be her sister.

When I approached the driver's side window to see if she wanted to fill-up, she asked, "I've got something under my brake pedal, can you check it out?"

"Sure will, ma'am. By the way, are you a movie star?"

She gave me a wink as she exited her car. She was wearing a full-length brown fur coat. But what surprised me were the bright-red high heels she had on despite the weather.

I leaned over, reached under the brake pedal and removed a squashed, overripe banana. After cleaning up the mess, I showed her the culprit and grabbed a paper towel so she could wipe off her shoe. She gave me a dollar tip along with a peck on the cheek that made me blush. She was the most glamorous woman I'd ever seen. I didn't wipe her lipstick off until the next morning.

A character, who hung out at the filling station, was a young army veteran named Artie. He lived nearby and knew the station manager. He asked me to go for a beer and I told him I wasn't old enough.

This led to my telling Artie, who had a crewcut and wore an olive-green Army field jacket, about my experience with not being old enough to join the grocery store union.

"I wish I had some ID to show I was twenty-one."

The next day Artie showed up with his military discharge papers showing his date of birth along with a copy of his driver's license.

"Here, you can use these for identification."

Although I kept his papers for some time, I never had the opportunity to use them.

My hernia was never far from my mind. As it got larger, it started to really bother me. At least a dozen times, I passed a doctor's office that was just two doors from my rooming house. The sign outside had "Dr." before a Polish name that was impossible to pronounce. Finally, I mustered the courage to go inside.

What would I tell the doctor? What would he say? I knew I was going to be embarrassed, that was a given.

I took a deep breath and walked into the waiting room that looked surprisingly warm, like a nice living room. It was late afternoon and I was the only patient there. A receptionist sat behind a glass window that she slid to the side. Her fingernails were long with dark purple nail polish and her fingers were twisted with arthritis like my grandmother's.

"Excuse me, Ma'am, I need to see the doctor."

"What's the matter? Do you have an appointment?"

The blood rushed to my face. I looked down so she might not notice how red I was and didn't say a word. She nodded and didn't press me for details.

"How old are you?"

"Eighteen." I lied.

"Have a seat and I'll tell him that you're waiting."

Soon a balding man in a white coat opened a door and called me in. He wore glasses. I guessed he was about my Dad's age.

With a nervous stutter, I explained how I'd ruptured myself doing my daily chores on a small farm. He listened carefully and asked me about my symptoms. I had to drop my drawers so he could examine me.

"Son, you have a severe hernia that is going to need surgery."

"I guess I knew that." I clumsily pulled up my underwear and pants.

"This is a serious condition. You should get that taken care of before it turns into an emergency situation."

He explained that if the intestine got stuck down there, it could burst and make me very sick. He offered to make arrangements for the hospital.

I nodded and quickly replied that my older sister would make the call.

Before leaving, I paid the receptionist fifteen dollars for the visit which I thought was very expensive.

I walked outside, looked up at the gray sky and sighed. Trying to put the matter out of my mind, I figured if I was careful, I could go on the way I was.

A week later Ethel and her family moved from their small apartment to a rented house about ten miles away in Homewood. The move prompted me to get a car so I could drive there to visit.

With the money I'd saved up from pumping gas, I bought a two-door 1948 Kaiser Special for ninety dollars at the nearby used-car lot. Happy to make a cash sale, the salesman didn't ask for any identification. I had no license and my only driver training consisted of a few miles in Dad's old pickup truck. The car didn't have any license plates.

As I got behind the wheel and started up, I hadn't gone a block when I saw a police car sitting opposite me at the traffic lights. The police officer did a U-turn and pulled around behind me while I was still stopped at the light.

He got out and approached my car.

"Can I see your license?"

"Don't have one, sir."

"Where did you get the car?"

"I just bought it and here are the papers."

He looked at the papers. After writing me a ticket he said, "Follow me to the police station." He pulled in front of me. We drove to the police station parking lot, a block away.

The officer accompanied me inside and walked me over to the desk sergeant.

"This young man has no driver's license and no plates."

The sergeant asked me a series of questions including my name, address, and who to call. I told him I was living with my sister and gave him Ethel's new phone number. It was Saturday and I hoped she'd be home.

"I have your brother here. He's been driving without a license, in an unregistered vehicle."

Within an hour but what seemed like an eternity, Ethel arrived at the police station. She was mad as hell. Jack and the kids waited in the car.

Ethel and I walked to the used-car lot where she took the bill of sale and title in hand and confronted the manager. I'd never seen Ethel's face so red.

"What'd you mean selling a car to a fourteen-year-old! Give him the ninety dollars back or I'll take you to court!" She thrust the papers into his chest.

"I didn't sell him the car but will deal with the salesman who did." The manager took a big step back.

Not only did Ethel get my money back but the car dealer had to pick up the Kaiser from the parking lot at the police station.

The next order of business was to pay the fifty-five-dollar fine. The police instructed us to see the City Judge whose office was two doors down from the police station.

We climbed the steps to the judge's office on the second floor. The judge looked remarkably like the one in Loudon County who put me on probation. He was tall, had white hair, and bushy eyebrows. The big difference was his northern accent.

I gave the judge three, twenty-dollar-bills. He reached into his pocket and pulled out a huge roll of money, peeling off a five-dollar bill, and handing it to me. He kept the ticket and we walked out.

When we left the judge's office, Ethel said she was feeling bad she'd left me in Harvey to fend for myself. She told me to move in with her in Homewood now that they had the space. I readily agreed and Jack drove us to the rooming house where I picked up my things. We stopped by the Road Chief station and let them know I was moving and had to give up my job.

In Homewood, I immediately got a job stocking shelves on Wednesdays and Thursdays at the IGA grocery store across the street from Ethel's new home. Needing more work, I also got a part-time job at the A&P supermarket on Fridays and Saturdays about four blocks away.

It was January 1957 and on the 26th day of the month, I turned fifteen years old.

On my birthday, my brother Joe took me to see the Harlem Globetrotters at Chicago Stadium.

Another time while Joe reported to Naval Reserves training in Gary, Indiana, I explored the Indiana Dunes State Park. I marveled at the fire from furnaces at the nearby steel mills reflected on the water of Lake Michigan. I couldn't believe how big Lake Michigan was. It looked like an endless cold ocean, not like the warm one I saw in Florida.

***

On these excursions Joe and I, who'd been basement roommates on Scott Avenue, reminisced about the times we spent together.

We roared when thinking about the day Joe, who was out of breath from a combination of running and pure unadulterated excitement, charged up the front lawn.

"Southern Dry Goods store has color TV! Color TV, COLOR TV!" Joe yelled as if he was the town crier.

I flew out the door at break-neck speed followed closely by David and Annie.

In less than five minutes running as fast as I could and out of breath, I reached Southern Dry Goods and made my way to the front row. A big crowd had gathered in front of the store's showcase window. We stared at the TVs.

As it turned out, the store had a clever way of advertising its TVs for sale. They dangled thin pieces of cellophane in different colors over the screens. The only thing visible beneath the colorful, transparent paper sheets—that blew from a fan squashed in the picture window—was the Indian head test pattern. Regular programming hadn't yet started for the day.

There was a run on colored cellophane after that. We even got some cellophane to drape over our TV.

Television viewing didn't sit well with Dad, who didn't like us wasting time. At first, Dad was intrigued by television but soon realized that while it was on, nothing was getting done around the house.

Early one evening, we were watching TV in the parlor while Dad was out working in the yard. When Dad came in, he saw us doing nothing. He got so damn mad, he walked in front of us, took out his pocketknife and whacked the end of the cord off. He demanded we get outside to do the chores and we scampered off in different directions.

A few days later when things settled down, we used electrical tape to repair the cord. But from that time on when Dad was home—the TV was off.

We studied TV broadcasts—whether sports, variety shows, news, or weather—in excruciating detail. Annie could spot anything and pointed out that the news anchor on WATV, who was reading the news from a sheet of paper, had dirty fingernails.

After a couple of months working in Homewood and due to the strain of stocking shelves and moving boxes, my hernia got even worse. My scrotum was swollen, painful, and was affecting the way I walked. When I laid down, the drooping segment of my intestine was no longer going back up—even when I pushed on it.

"Connie, are you all right?" Ethel asked when my discomfort became too great to hide. My face wrenched in pain as I finally told her what was going on.

"No, I haven't been feeling well. I hurt myself slopping the hogs at Dry Gap Pike a while back and the pain is getting worse." It was about all the detail that I wanted to share. But I also knew that Ethel was the mother of boys so she'd understand my reluctance to discuss private matters. I told her what the doctor said about surgery.

"I am going to send you back to Mom and Dad to get that taken care of," Ethel said. She wasted no time in calling Don as neither one of us had the money for me to get back to Knoxville.

A few days later, Don bought me a plane ticket and mailed it to Ethel along with a five-dollar bill for my travel money. Jack drove me to Midway Airport but it was the wrong airport. When we realized the mistake, we made our way to O'Hare that had recently opened. I just made my flight.

Although I'd been to the McGhee-Tyson airport in Knoxville to see planes land and take off, I'd never flown before. I had a grand time on the plane, looking out the windows at the clouds, and enjoying a snack. The excitement of flying took my mind off leaving Chicago, my hernia, and the life I'd had there. I thought about what I'd missed at home. Fishing, squirrel hunting, the Smoky Mountains, grits, and sweet tea came to mind.

When I landed, I took the Maryville bus from the airport to Gay Street in Knoxville and then caught the KTL bus to Scott Avenue. I walked with the small suitcase Ethel gave me to Betty's. Betty and Glen drove me out to Dry Gap Pike later that day.

My parents knew about my health condition from Ethel and Don so I didn't have to tell them. Unlike my excursions to New Orleans and Cincinnati, this time they knew where I'd been.

Within a couple of days, I saw a family doctor who set me up for surgery at St. Mary's Hospital where I stayed for three days. I was forced to drink a huge glass of orange juice with castor oil. What an awful way to ruin orange juice! I managed to gulp it down. I also remember the black orderly named Pop who prepped me by shaving the hair off my genitals the night before surgery, jokingly saying, "Don't worry, I won't cut it off."

The nurses had me up and walking the next day.

My immediate reaction to the surgery was a huge sense of relief. In what had seemed like forever, I didn't have to think about my hernia anymore.

Chapter Ten

BACK TO SCHOOL

H anging around the house while recuperating wasn't my idea of a good time. But it was a blessing Dad still worked the 3 p.m. to 11 p.m. shift.

While Dad cut me some slack, I was still uneasy when he was around. All us kids spent our youth on tenterhooks expecting his explosion of anger at any moment.

The doctor's prescription included walking, not hitching. Early one evening I headed to Earl Graves' store where Earl was glad to see me despite the fact I took off after he vouched for my character with the judge. Word had traveled that I'd had an operation.

"Hey Conley, how ya' doing? You're looking a bit peaky but that's no wonder."

In addition to our accents, East Tennesseans shared a passion for health talk. No detail about an operation or illness was considered off limits.

Earl told me about how hernias ran in his family and how his uncle, who had since passed, had the biggest rupture this side of the Tennessee River. The blood drained from my face when Earl described him as a huge man needing a special truss.

"His hernia belt was the size of Love's Creek Road underpass!" he roared, giving me a slap on the back.

I didn't laugh. I really wanted to put this hernia thing behind me.

So when a neighbor, Rufus Cupp, came in, I tried to change the subject so my recovery wouldn't turn into a three-way conversation. He'd surely heard about my operation.

"Can you give me a lift?" I asked.

Rufus said he had plans for a quick stop at the Polka Dot Club with his girlfriend, Dollie Sue. But I could go along and keep her teenage daughter Hazelene company while they grabbed a beer.

Dollie Sue was a divorcee. Divorced women were rare and had the reputation for being fast. While most men were church-going folks, some secretly looked at Rufus with envy.

Eager to escape Earl's store, I climbed into the back seat next to Hazelene, who lived in an apartment with her mother. We drove to the Polka Dot Club in front of the Broadway Speedway.

While they went inside, Hazelene—a big country gal—put the moves on me. She wanted to smooch and more. Her breath smelled like peaches; no surprise, as I spotted a fresh pit in the ashtray. I might've lost my virginity that night except for the bruising and stitches down there causing me to yell out.

"Stop! That hurts! There's no way I can do this."

Hazelene flinched and jumped back, pulling her hand out of my pants.

I showed her the bruises and stitches covered in Mercurochrome. She wrinkled her nose and mumbled, "Gross!"

The next time I saw Hazelene she was coming out of church with another boy and to my relief, ignored me.

It wasn't long before I'd fully recovered but there wasn't enough of the 1956-1957 school year left to bother with.

Always looking for work, I saw the door was open at Calvin Copeland's cabinet shop on Dry Gap Pike and Beaverdam Road, and stopped in.

Calvin, who was about fifteen years older than me, was building a twelve-foot wooden, ski boat. Having an interest in woodworking and carpentry, I continued to check on the status of the boat and help Calvin out. He always found something for me to do and explained in detail how to safely and thoroughly complete a task.

After a while, I looked up to Calvin. He had a countrified accent and didn't talk a lot but when he did, his words had meaning. He called me "Stick" because I'd stick with a task until done and taught me about patience—something my Dad lacked.

He gave me a part-time job at his filling station where I learned more about cars and running a business. The sign over at the door said: "Treat every customer like they're the only one you got."

At home I was busy helping Dad, Bill, and David build hog and chicken pens, plant a large vegetable garden, and build a small shed for the milking cow. Long, hot, buggy workdays were the norm.

Once Dad went to work, I'd take off fishing at Beaver Creek or grab the single-shot 410-gauge shotgun for squirrel and rabbit hunting along Beaver Ridge.

About 200 yards from the bridge on Dry Gap Pike that crossed Beaver Creek was our swimming hole with a huge tree that leaned over. It had an old wire cable with wooden handle attached that we'd swing on like Tarzan. As often as twice a day on hot days, a bunch of us boys would strip off and jump in naked as j-birds. For my pals, who had no indoor plumbing, it was the only way to take a bath.

We were always looking for ways to make a buck. We picked wild blackberries from bushes along the banks of the creek and sold them for seventy-five cents a gallon.

At fifteen, I was too young to quit school. But I wasn't allowed to go back until I took a series of placement tests. I reported to the Knox County Superintendent's Office where a psychologist could also assess my mental health.

The shrink had on a red sweater with white reindeers that distracted me. He told me his mother knit it for him. But it was still hot outside and wasn't close to Christmas. I couldn't figure out why he was wearing it. Maybe he was the type of guy that didn't embarrass easy.

He told me to draw on a piece of paper how to find something of value I'd lost on the football field. I imagined losing a ring, though I didn't own one. My diagram had grids dividing up the field. I explained I'd search grid-by-grid until I found the ring. I'm pretty sure I nailed the test. The shrink seemed impressed.

He also asked me a bunch of questions like "What makes you happy?" "Are things okay at home?" "Do you like school?"

There was nothing deep about my answers. I was honest. I was happier hunting squirrels, pitching hay, or playing football than I ever was at home.

He nodded so I guessed he agreed because he gave me an official-looking paper that cleared me for school.

Rather than return to Powell High, I opted to reenroll at Halls High School. Having missed most of my freshman year, I was placed back a year in the ninth grade with the Class of 1961.

There was a maturity about me that other freshmen hadn't yet grown into. For one thing I was a year older, taller, and heavier than they were. Due to my exploits and travels, I was well known around town.

Some kids said I looked kind of like Johnny Cash whose record "I Walk the Line" was topping the charts.

Being friendly came naturally to me. It'd served me well whether selling hotdogs or hitching a ride.

In my first week, there was an assembly for the freshman class to elect a slate of class officers. The students sitting near me started encouraging me to stand for president.

"Come on, Conley, you'd be great," a classmate said.

"You nominate me and I'll run."

My name was put on the slate that was elected unanimously. I didn't know what to think. Politics wasn't something I'd ever thought about. If President Eisenhower was speaking on TV, we turned it off. He was ancient and boring.

I hadn't thought it possible but I was starting to like school.

But when it came to academics, I did just enough to get a passing grade.

I signed up for Algebra I, English, civics, art, and gym. I also enrolled in vocational agriculture that included carpentry, welding, electrical work, and ironwork— any skills that could be used on a farm. Being naturally athletic, gym was my favorite class.

Signing up for Algebra was a mistake. Luckily, I realized that right away and was able to drop that course and take general math.

Although I wasn't a good student, I got along with my teachers. Being popular was not something I'd sought but, now that I was radioactive, I enjoyed the attention.

Through vocational agriculture, I became a member of the Future Farmers of America. My teacher appointed me to serve as the FFA chapter reporter. I also helped at the FFA concession stand that year and sold popcorn during school basketball games to raise money for club activities.

Someone suggested we needed more advertising about popcorn sales. Eager to help, I offered to make a stencil in art class that we'd use to paint "popcorn" on gym walls. I made the stencil but didn't realize I'd mistakenly spelled "popocorn" (with the extra "o").

Using my stencil, I took it upon myself to paint the wall opposite the gym bleachers. After school, I made several bright-red "popocorn" signs about fifteen feet apart. The letters were big enough to be seen from the stands.

It was the girls' physical education teacher, who pointed out the misspelling the next day when I was cutting through the gym to admire my work.

"Conley, come here a minute," said Miss Drinnen, who also taught science and reading. She wasn't known for a sense of humor.

"Do you see anything wrong with your spelling?"

Admittedly, I couldn't see the mistake.

"Huh?" I asked.

"Firstly, please address me using my name and secondly, popcorn is misspelled."

"Sorry, Miss Drinnen, I meant no disrespect." I felt myself blush as my eyes desperately searched back and forth across "popocorn" trying to find the error. *What is she talking about?* But thank God, someone was looking out for me because I caught the extra "o" as I spelled the word letter-by-letter in my head just before she could point it out.

I recovered my composure in time to fib that I wrote it that way on purpose to get people's attention.

"Just like you, Miss Drinnen, basketball fans of all ages will be staring at 'popocorn' and talking about how it's spelled wrong. It'll be a topic of discussion and generate more sales! I can even see parents asking their younger kids if they know the right way to spell popcorn!" I talked fast so she couldn't interrupt.

"Really, Conley?" Miss Drinnen said, but I knew she wasn't looking for an answer. "Go to class." She shook her head and turned around sharply on her high heels. I could hear the click of her shoes on the gym floor growing distant as she walked to her office.

"Popocorn" adorned the gym wall for the rest of my freshman year and beyond. From that point forward, I became fanatical about spelling and the dictionary became my friend.

∞∞∞∞∞∞∞∞∞∞∞∞∞∞∞∞∞∞∞∞∞∞∞∞∞∞∞∞∞

Unbeknownst to Dad, I went out for football and having some size to me, I was a starter on the varsity. David had graduated and was past the point of turning me in. If I was careful, Dad wouldn't find out. Even if he had, he couldn't have stopped me—he was having too many problems of his own.

Dad's persistent psoriasis was flaring up; he had unsightly scabs behind his ears and knees and on his forearms. His coworkers at the railroad didn't want to be around him. Thinking his condition was contagious, they refused to sit in a chair he'd sat in. I was ashamed of the way Dad looked and couldn't muster any compassion for him.

Dad kept all his prescriptions in an old fruitcake tin. He'd call to Mom, "Cora, bring me *all* my medicine! Bring me *all* my medicine!"

There were only sixteen players on my team so many of us played on both sides of the ball. I played center on offense and linebacker on defense.

We played Fulton High School at Shield Watkins Field in Knoxville for Fulton's homecoming game. Fulton was a city school and there were forty on the team not including coaches and managers.

When we charged onto the gridiron, there was a loud "wha…" sound coming from the packed Fulton bleachers that almost drowned out the cheers from the Halls side. The bewildered Fulton fans wondered where the rest of our team was. Then their team and entourage stormed onto the field. Raucous applause from the home crowd was nearly drowned out by the beat of the drums and crash of cymbals from the impressive school band.

Fulton beat us badly. We didn't score. But Halls got half the gate receipts to buy supplies for the team.

After the game, the Halls Boosters Club bought us steak dinners at the Lucky Clover restaurant in Halls Crossroads. A juicy steak was a real treat.

<hr/>

On a drizzly, dreary fall afternoon after a mid-week football practice, I cut through the Avondale Farms Creamery pasture to hook up with Joyce Yearout. Her father was a dairyman and they lived at the farm.

Joyce, who snuck out of her house to meet me, was a freshman too. The two of us had been making eyes at each other in the corridors and cafeteria. She was a cute girl with dirty blonde hair, an engaging smile, and classy chassis.

I waited in the barn for about five minutes before she showed up. We kissed clumsily as we sat together on the straw-covered floor with our backs against the first row of haybales. She wore the sweetest single-drop pearl necklace that hung down just above her rack. I checked it out as our lips pressed.

From our vantage point we could see Joyce's house. After fifteen minutes, the porch light came on which was the signal that Joyce better go inside.

It was about 6:30 p.m. as I headed home, walking with the traffic on Maynardville Pike. My feet seemed to fly along the gravel shoulder as I strode toward the end of Cunningham Road where I planned to hitch a ride. My teenage mind was on a natural high about my new girlfriend, football, and friends. Heck, I was tall, handsome, and popular. Life seemed pretty darn good.

Then holy cow! A whack, a thud, and darkness! The next thing I remember was slowly opening my eyes to see a crowd hovering over me, asking if I was okay.

I was lying faceup in the middle of the road directly opposite Norris Food Market whose store lights illuminated the highway. I later found out a panel truck hit me from behind, launching me six feet into the air and over the hood. I had on my FFA jacket but was knocked right out of my shoes. Some days later when I put my jacket back on, there was still straw in the pockets from my rendezvous with Joyce in the feed barn.

The only thing I recall about the accident, apart from the flashing lights, was a group of strange people staring down at me before I passed out again. It was like a black-and-white movie. There was no color in any of their faces or clothing. Their voices sounded like they were in an echo chamber. I didn't appear to be bleeding anywhere but my legs felt funny.

In and out of consciousness as I was loaded into the ambulance to St. Mary's Hospital, I briefly heard the siren. The next time I "came to" was in the emergency room where I was concussed and kept asking for Pop, the orderly who had prepped me for my hernia surgery. That confused the emergency room nurses who thought I was asking for my father. Pop wasn't working that day, but my Dad did show up in the ER and I remember him saying, "I'm here, Connie."

I became upset and unruly when I heard the doctors saying I needed a cystoscopy. Because it was to be performed "down there" to check for internal injuries, I thought they meant castration. Having castrated boars at Black Oak Ridge, I was frightened at the thought. A nice nurse explained what a cystoscopy was and why it was needed. It was a painful procedure and it hurt to pee for the next couple of days.

The next afternoon, a parade of classmates came to the hospital. They were surprised to see me up and making jokes. The accident had increased my celebrity as it was written up in the *Knoxville News Sentinel* with the headline: "Halls High gridder hit by truck."

If Dad—who hadn't abandoned his objection to sports—saw or heard about the newspaper story, he never mentioned it. Even if he had, there was no way I would've given up football. I think he knew that.

I was bruised and sore all over but the doctors determined I had no broken bones. I had to stay in the hospital for three days for observation.

When I returned to school, I got a huge welcome. Everywhere I went in the building, students, faculty and staff—even the cafeteria workers—asked how I was doing. Some said they had been praying for me and started prayer chains on my behalf.

My hip bothered me for a couple of weeks. I had to sit out the following week's game but I was cleared to return to football practice. While I'd never have wished to be hit by a truck again, I was overwhelmed with the attention and concern for my welfare. I didn't appreciate how close I'd come to being killed.

The truckdriver who hit me worked for a wholesale tobacco distributor. He didn't stop but had to pull over a quarter of a mile down the road due to a blown tire. The impact of hitting me knocked out a headlight and the right front fender was bent against the wheel.

My brother Ray handled the insurance claim which resulted in a payout of several thousand dollars that Dad used to pay bills. Dad also bought four acres of undeveloped land on Long Holler Road to build a retirement home.

That winter, my pals and I liked to hang out at Clem White's garage at the end of Cunningham Road across from the school bus stop. Clem did mechanical work and lived in one end of the garage.

We sat on some old car seats warming up around the stove. These gatherings were a way for us to talk about guy-stuff including girls, sports, and cars.

While I was generally a good, hardworking boy—I was still up for adventure and a good time—even if it wasn't entirely legal.

When fancy hubcaps came up and how they could be sold for two dollars apiece to a junkyard on Oak Ridge Highway, we were all in. We equated stealing hubcaps with something as small as stealing a watermelon or siphoning gas; wrongdoings that we didn't consider to be criminal acts.

We decided to head over to the Sharon Baptist Church on Pedigo Road, knowing it was prayer night and the parking lot would be full.

Four of us including Clem's brother Loyal, who was driving, jumped into his maroon Studebaker and drove to the church that was less two miles away.

"Make sure they are singing before you pop the hubcaps because they might hear us," Loyal said, as we inched in without headlights.

It was dark except for lights coming from the church. We could hear the congregation singing even though the sanctuary windows were closed. The chorus took a break, perhaps to find the right page in the hymnal. We waited for the singing to resume to muffle any noise. I popped two fancy hubcaps off a '56 Chrysler.

Loyal put his hubcaps on the floorboard in the backseat and the rest of us held the ones we stole on our laps. We drove back to Clem's garage and I walked home, covering my two hubcaps with leaves under the honeysuckle bushes by my driveway. Clem knew nothing about our goings-on.

By the next morning, the word got out about who was responsible. The father of one of our group knew someone at the church who recognized Loyal's car. We were told to leave the hubcaps at Clem's and no one would press charges. That afternoon, we brought the hubcaps to the garage and they were returned to their rightful owners. Nothing more was said.

———

I got my driver's license right after I turned sixteen in January. By early June when school let out, Dad gave me $170 from the insurance settlement from the hit-and-run accident to buy an old car. While I was grateful for the money, I knew Dad kept the rest of the insurance payout to buy the land at Long Holler.

I paid $100 for a royal-blue, two-door, 1949 Ford sedan in the back row of a used-car lot on Oldham and Central avenues in North Knoxville. The rest went for my car insurance.

Filled with pride in my new wheels, I puttied the rusted-out holes and repainted the rusty rocker panels under both doors. My car had a V-8 flathead engine with a manual transmission and a six-volt electrical system.

I put an old light-blue, hobnail chenille bedspread on the soiled front bench seat and ordered sixteen-inch black-wall tires through the Spiegel Catalog. Months later, I added white Portawall inserts, turning them into mock whitewalls. I painted the rims fire-engine red and removed the hubcaps.

I installed a suicide knob on the steering wheel to make steering easier using only my right hand. I repaired the hole in the muffler by cutting the metal from a tin can and wrapping a wire around it. The radio antenna was broken off at its base so I straightened out a coat hanger and stuck it in the hole.

Gas cost twenty-nine cents a gallon. If my tank was half-full, I thought I was rich.

While taking off in low gear and speed-shifting to second while practicing my drag-racing skills, I tore a couple of teeth off the cluster gear by popping the clutch too fast. After that I'd take off in second gear until I earned enough money to get the transmission fixed.

My car taught me how to be a shade-tree mechanic picking up used parts in junkyards. When my starter went on the blink—I'd park my car on a hill, turn the key, put it in second gear, and wait for a push. After a couple of months, I located a used starter and changed it out myself. My dimmer switch on the floor went out so I had to short circuit my headlights so the high-beams stayed on when the lights were on.

With my AM radio blaring with my favorite hit "The Ballad of Thunder Road" by Robert Mitchum—I was Mr. Cool. Maynardville Pike (Highway 33) was nicknamed Thunder Road because bootleggers traveled it as they transported whiskey to Knoxville. Beer was legal but hard liquor was not.

When Uncle Walton visited Mom, he'd ride to Knoxville along Thunder Road with the Evarts, Kentucky undertaker in a hearse stocked with moonshine.

I drove around with my left elbow resting half-out the open driver's side window and my right hand on the suicide knob.

My favorite hangout was the Blue Circle, about four miles away in Fountain City, where there were stalls for a dozen cars served by the carhops. We picked up girls there and showed off by driving our cars completely around the Blue Circle.

At times it got ridiculous with cars circling ten or twelve times. Hamburgers were twelve-cents, so I could treat myself and a girl to hamburgers and Cokes for less than a dollar.

Chapter Eleven

SOPHOMORE SUMMER

It was a bitch being held back a year. Most of my buddies were in the Class of 1960 and I wanted to be with them. It was embarrassing explaining why I wasn't a dumb-ass. But I hated going into the whole thing about being arrested and running-off. I'd put all that behind me.

It was a real bummer to learn I wouldn't be eligible for football my senior year with the Class of '61 because of my age. That was enough motivation for me to sign up for summer school and take the subject I dreaded most: English.

"Conley, you can graduate on time by taking five courses the next two years—but the only thing missing is a year of English." Principal Myers explained I couldn't double up on English. "Make that up and you should be all set."

"Gee whiz, thanks Mr. Myers! I think I can handle that."

"Go down to the Guidance Office and they'll fix you up."

If principals were all like Mr. Myers, they weren't that bad. He was looking out for me.

Nearly tripping over my feet, I ran out into the hall and around the corner to guidance. The floors had just been polished so my shoes let off a loud squeal when they skidded sideways to a stop at the office door. The centrifugal force sent my books flying across the hall. I gathered them up, stuffed any loose papers into my math book, took a deep breath, and knocked on the door.

I'd never been to Miss McGuire's office so I tried to make an impression by looking her right in the eyes. But I was unable to avoid staring at her glasses that had these sparkly rhinestones on the part that curved up over her eyebrows, so I extended my hand.

"Miss McGuire, my name is Conley Ford and I need to talk to you about summer school."

"Take a seat and let's see what I can do," she said with a half-smile.

Patience wasn't one of my glowing character traits so I did my best to listen to Miss McGuire while she lectured me about the challenges of summer school and taking a bigger course load next fall. I had trouble keeping that left leg still. It always jiggled when I was edgy about something.

She explained I was in the general education track, not college prep, so I might be able to handle the extra class. I'd have to work hard. I nodded in agreement. If there was one thing, I wasn't the least bit highfalutin' about, it was where I fit in terms of academics. Being a brain wasn't high on my agenda.

After my enthusiastic reassurances about the importance of uninterrupted attendance, she signed a letter allowing me to take sophomore English that was offered at West High in West Knoxville. It was an eight-week-long course, meeting half days and started just a week after school was out.

There was only a month left of my freshman year and it flew by. And before I knew it, I was headed to summer school. To help with expenses, I used my super-friendly personality to charm shy, identical twin sisters, Judy and Joanie, who were in the same English class and needed transportation. I offered to drive them back 'n' forth in my '49 Ford for fifty cents a day, covering my gas and more. They talked mostly in annoying giggles but readily agreed to hire me as their driver.

In my family, there was one set of twins: my brother Don and sister Dana. Other than sharing a birthday, they were nothing alike.

But Judy and Joanie were like something I'd never seen. Apart from wearing different colored ponytail ribbons, they dressed alike. They even had the same voice. Believe me, I have an eye for detail, but it was impossible to tell them apart. The girls got a kick out of my never knowing for sure who was who and often answered me at the same time. I got used to it. They always rode in the back so I figured if I ever became a chauffeur this was good training.

Our class had no homework which was a relief since I wouldn't have done it anyway. The English teacher was younger and nicer than any I'd encountered. She said no one would flunk her class as long as we came every day and paid attention. I knew I could deal with that.

In the meantime, at home Crit Cox— who lived behind us and had an old truck and a couple of mules— asked Dad about cutting down the stand of tall pine trees at the back end of our property and selling the lumber.

Dad planned to clear the land anyway so he worked a deal with Crit to get one-third of the milled lumber and

Crit could have the rest. No money needed to change hands.

When it came to neighbors, Crit was as good as any. Crit let me work for him snaking logs into the sawmill the previous summer but I was lousy at handling a mule in the woods.

Dad used our portion of the lumber Crit cut down for a very basic two-room dwelling beside our one-acre garden. David, Bill, and I comprised the construction crew and worked our asses off in the hot sun. My brothers and I wired the house for electricity and ran water to the structure; it had no indoor toilet but could use our outhouse.

For some unknown reason mosquitoes love me. They were always on attack and seemed to leave my brothers alone. I told myself that I must have tastier blood, a revolting thought. One night, I counted seventy mosquito bites and those were just the ones I could see.

It is hard to explain how our Dad still had control over us. David and I were as big as grown men. But Dad had a way of making us feel small. His controlling nature took over even the simplest tasks. Whether it was grabbing the wrong-sized nail or the wrong way to swing a hammer, we heard about it. When Bill got frustrated, he would just storm off, go inside and stare at the wall. With Bill's mental condition, Dad left him alone.

It wasn't always easy but I was getting pretty good at tuning Dad out and finding recognition and support outside my family.

Before Joe left when we lived on Scott Avenue, I remember the time Joe was late getting home. Dad made him write "Where is my wandering boy tonight?" ten thousand times. It took him the whole summer. Joe tried using two pencils balanced between his fingers at the same time to write in duplicate.

Why didn't Joe just tear up the paper and say, "No!" None of us could ever explain why standing up to Dad was so hard.

<hr/>

Crit, seeing our small building go up, asked Dad if it was available because his sister-in-law Maggie needed a place to live. She was living with her husband and son in an apartment on top of Happy Bradley's Store on Emory Road and had to move out.

As the story goes, Maggie answered an ad on the radio placed by Cecil "Toe-Joe" Fox, who was looking for a wife. Toe-Joe and Maggie, who were in their thirties, then met up and following a short courtship, got hitched, and had Dooney.

Toe-Joe was a little guy who couldn't talk clearly due to a poorly mended broken jaw, and Maggie couldn't talk clearly due to a cleft palate. Toe-Joe, who always carried a red can of Prince Albert smoking tobacco in his bib overalls pocket with a pack of rolling papers, was good with a team of mules and often worked for Crit.

Toe-Joe, Maggie, and Dooney, who was about five, moved into our tiny dwelling, rent-free with the understanding Maggie would help Mom out in the garden and in the house if needed.

On Toe-Joe's payday, the family shopped at Earl Graves Store to buy groceries. Toe-Joe, squawking, "We'll eat today and starve tomorrow!", brought the goods back in a box on his shoulders with Maggie beside him. Dooney, chewing on a piece of candy, trailed behind. I couldn't figure out why Toe-Joe bought things like canned green beans when we had a garden full.

<hr />

That same summer it seemed like every time I pulled up in my bucket of bolts at a traffic light in Fountain City on my way to and from Halls, the teen driver in the car beside me would rev his engine and want to race. The encounters never lasted longer than a few hundred yards and were dependent on lack of traffic. My old Ford never won but it was always worth a try.

On Friday and Saturday nights, the straightaway on Maynardville Pike passing in front of Mayes Texaco, Bayles Boat Repair, and the Lucky Clover restaurant— became a quarter-mile drag strip.

After the businesses closed, challengers from all over the area fancied how their fast, souped-up cars would compete along that stretch of road. We were in awe of these guys—who were in their twenties and were in a different class than us teens firing up our jalopies.

Mayes Brothers Texaco was closed after 10 p.m. except for the wrecker service which was operated by Big Red, who was in competition with Smut Smith of Fountain City Wrecker Service. Big Red had a police radio so he could hear about breakdowns as they happened and be first on the scene.

The racing started in front of the Texaco station and ended at the intersection with Cunningham Road. Upwards of forty people stood around the gas pumps to watch the competition and the crowd could hear the radio that alerted them to any approaching police cars.

Sometimes there was betting about who would be the fastest. As the first race started, exhaust permeated the humid air. Pesky gnats that love sticky weather kept us all batting the space around our faces to keep them away.

The normal drag race consisted of two cars racing down and not racing back. One hot August night for some unexplained reason, the two cars turned around to race back as two others took off at the start.

We could hear the screech of brakes before the explosive boom of crushing steel and braking glass when three of the four cars collided at the intersection. The driver from Halls Crossroads was killed and two others were severely injured. The fourth driver was able to veer off down Cunningham Road and escaped injury.

Spectators' screams turned to a dead silence—even the gnats stopped buzzing.

The accident felt like a gut punch. The blood drained from my face as I ran to the side of the filling station, bent over, and barfed. I didn't know the racer from Halls personally, but I'd seen him around town.

I kept thinking how he was smiling and talking before hopping into the driver's seat through the window of his cream-colored, '49 Olds Rocket 88. He flicked his cigarette out the window, grinned, and gave a short salute to the spectators before flooring the gas pedal. The remains of his Camel smoke still lay there in the road.

Big Red towed the wrecked cars to Mayes Brothers Texaco where ambulances, fire engines, and police all showed up.

The crash prompted the building of a dragstrip adjacent to the Broadway Speedway, the professional racecar track in Halls Crossroads. But the new strip didn't deter road-racing for long.

Within a month, the weekend-night drag racing resumed but moved about five miles away to the Norris Freeway to an area called Big Pine that got its name from the big pine tree at the start. The straightaway was about a mile long.

People would still congregate at the Texaco station at night and when a race was on, would jump in cars and take off. As many as twenty-five to thirty cars went to Big Pine to watch.

The last drag race I saw that summer was between popular driver Pete Blazer in a 1955 Buick Century and a guy from South Knoxville who had a Harley motorcycle. He challenged Pete to a race. Surprising to us hotrod fans, the Harley edged the Buick Century at the finish line.

At the end of that summer, I found out I'd succeeded in skipping my sophomore year altogether. I was reclassified as a junior and back on track with the Class of 1960.

At home, Dad was having more problems with his health. He was taking sick days and missing a lot of work.

With his seniority, Dad was the chief call clerk at the railroad yard office scheduling the train crews. But accounting and administration was becoming more advanced. Dad struggled with the new system and preferred to work the old-fashioned way, writing everything down with an indelible pencil. Dad had a knot on his index finger from holding those pencils to keep track of the boxcars and write his reports.

The pencils stand out in my memory and not for a positive reason. When I was about eight, Dad cottoned onto the fact there was no school that day. He was working days and could use my help.

At first, I was pretty cool about it. He taught me how to tell if a boxcar was empty by hitting the side of the car with a hammer. If there was a bellowing sound it was empty—a dead thud meant it was not.

After a while, he shared his lunch that Mom had packed in a thermos. We split a pinto bean sandwich on light bread. Dad peeled an apple with his pocketknife and gave me half.

"Connie, take these pencils and sharpen them," Dad said pointing to a large, hand-crank sharpener on the wall.

Then he climbed up onto his huge desk, curled up, and took a nap. I shrugged my shoulders and guessed the desk was as good a place as any to lie down.

While he snoozed, I held the pencils in my mouth while sharpening them one by one. There were about twenty pencils and I tackled them in three shifts.

When I was done, I used the restroom. What I saw in the mirror was horrifying! Purple dye from the pencils was all over my tongue and mouth. I panicked and used all the paper towels. Then I resorted to toilet paper. But no amount of scrubbing with soap and water helped. Walking around with a purple mouth for a week was mortifying.

I could always count on finding comfort with Betty. Before she was married and still lived at home, she had a job at the White Stores in the Holler. When I stopped in on Saturdays, she'd give me a dime for the matinee at Center Theater, better known as the Rat Hole.

I'd never seen a rat there but had no reason to doubt first-hand accounts of the critters running under seats and stealing popcorn. Just in case, I'd prop my feet on the chair in front of me.

It was the Saturday after my pencil trouble. The purple had faded to a gray shadow encircling my mouth. Betty handed me a shiny new dime to see "A Ticket to Tomahawk." She knew how I loved cowboy movies, even musical ones. Admission was nine cents. I had a penny left over for Kits Taffy.

The previews were on. As I got comfortable with my feet up, I bit into a piece of Kits Taffy. Holy Cow! The candy glued itself to a molar that'd been harboring a cavity. I couldn't dislodge it. The pain was more than I could bear and I ran home crying. After the taffy melted away, the ache was still there. Mom gave me an aspirin to put on my tooth.

It wasn't my week.

Chapter Twelve

SENIOR YEAR

It was a couple of weeks before school when my buddy Joe Henderlight and me, armed with shotguns for rabbit hunting, headed out on a damp August morning.

On these excursions, we'd walk quietly along fence lines, where the grass was longer, to coax the rabbits out of hiding.

The sun had just come up. I was driving my '49 Ford along a bumpy, one-lane gravel cart path into the woods. Single-lane roads twist like snakes through the trees in the foothills of the Smoky Mountains. Thoughts of our moms' fried rabbit—a nice change from chicken–made our mouths water. We knew how to skin rabbits and use their fur to stuff in our unlined leather work gloves for the winter. Sometimes, we kept a rabbit's foot for good luck.

We pulled onto a tiny wooden bridge over a stream. I was a pretty good driver but bald tires on wet wood is never good. Maybe I was going a little too fast.

We both yelled as we skidded off, hitting a tree stump.

I knew from the cracking sound that my car was toast. I took a look. The A-frame underneath the right wheel had snapped. "Damn it!"

We were miles from the nearest house. With our shotguns over our shoulders, it took about two hours to trudge back to Joe's.

While we walked, Joe talked about his dream of playing in the National Football League.

"I'll be there to root you on." I couldn't imagine playing a sport for a job. But if anybody could do it, Joe could.

Joe and I were football teammates. I was a good player, but Joe was a star. The same could be said for his abilities on the basketball court and baseball diamond. Years later he had a stint with the Atlanta Falcons.

Tall and sandy-haired, Joe looked like Kookie in the TV show, *77 Sunset Strip*. He was an only child and his parents allowed him to do pretty much whatever he wanted. Unlike me, he wasn't tied to endless chores or work.

"How 'bout you? What do you want to do?"

"Dunno." I'd been focused on living day-to-day and hadn't allowed myself to dream. "Just trying to get through school, I guess."

I changed the subject to meeting girls at the Blue Circle. Whenever Joe borrowed his mother's snazzy, two-tone, yellow and black 1956 Chevy Bel Air, girls flocked to his car. We pooled our resources and bought them chocolate malts.

Once back at Joe's house, he grabbed the keys to his mother's car and drove me to Mayes Brothers Texaco where Big Red agreed to tow my car. I climbed into his truck.

Big Red knew the back roads better than I did. The dirt roads were so narrow that tree branches scraped Big Red's truck that was already marked up pretty bad. He just shook his head when he saw the shape my car was in.

He towed my Ford to Dry Gap Pike and only asked for five dollars. I didn't question the amount; Big Red knew my family had no money. I borrowed the fiver from Bill, who always carried his wallet even though he never went anywhere or bought anything.

My car sat beside our driveway for a couple of weeks until I sold it to Clem White for parts. I wasn't in a rush to sell it, although I could use the money. Letting it go tore into me. There was no way I could get enough cash to replace it. My first car, along with the memories, was going to be reduced to a pile of junk.

When the school year got underway, I resumed my role as an outgoing, popular kid. School days beat being home by a mile. And to top it off, I was in love.

The first time I saw Patsy Drummonds was at the end of the summer when I still had my car. She was walking with another girl I knew. I caught up to them and made her acquaintance. She was a freshman, a majorette, and one of the prettiest girls I'd ever seen.

We soon hooked up, held hands, and talked. She had just moved to town, had two older brothers, and had never heard of a family as big as mine.

I think Patsy liked having a big senior as a boyfriend. She agreed to be my girl and go steady. Seeing Patsy wearing my Varsity letter sweater around school made me feel like a million bucks.

On dates, Patsy's father let me take his two-door Chevrolet Biscayne. She had to be back home by nine. Her parents and brothers liked me a lot. When I could get away, I loved hanging out at Patsy's. She had a nice family that got along together. At her house, things were calm and relaxed. I didn't know families could be like that.

Adding excitement to my senior year, Halls High planned to hold elections for student council. Students in all four grades would vote by paper ballot.

A classmate offered to nominate me for student body president if he could serve as my campaign manager. I readily agreed. Having been president of the Class of '61 in my freshman year, I thought I'd have a leg up on the competition. But I expected a close race as my opponent was more academically inclined than me and was a star basketball player.

My team spent the week before the election campaigning that included making posters and plastering the school with the message "You want something done, Conley's the one!" Since I'd taken art every year, some of my fellow art students made signs for me.

I ran on the platform of school beautification and during an assembly, gave a talk about how to "field strip" a cigarette butt to cut down on litter. I demonstrated peeling off the paper and crumbling the tobacco with my fingers before grinding it into the ground with my foot. The audience applauded and laughed. I grinned, pulled out a handkerchief, and bent down to pick up the ground-up tobacco from the stage floor. Absorbing the ovation, I gave a short bow before asking for votes, waving broadly, and striding off the stage.

My campaign bio included my record from the prior year working with the art class repainting the school marquee and assisting the Halls Boosters Club selling tickets for a horse show. The proceeds went to buy an electrified scoreboard for the football field.

With the help of the FFA, I led a group of students planting shrubs and dogwood trees along the side of the school driveway next to Emory Road. We also painted the wooden posts by the school entrance. These landscaping efforts were recognized in a feature story in the *Knoxville News Sentinel* about local school news.

The school-wide vote was held on a Friday, and I waited around with my campaign team for the results. It wasn't even close. I was elected student body president. I leapt into the air when I heard the news.

The result prompted Principal Myers, to remark, "Conley, you never cease to amaze me!"

The dramatic club, of which I was a member, formed a Thespian Society chapter. The Thespians staged a couple of plays before the school audience.

Ironically, one time I played a lawyer debating a case and another time, I played a prisoner named Ace who had to report to the warden. Being in front of people came naturally to me and I wasn't afraid to adlib. If I wasn't on stage, I worked on stage props.

But the polish of high school wore off as the second half of the year got underway. A case of senioritis settled in. Along with my classmates, I started to think about what would happen after high school. I'd never received any encouragement or direction from my parents. My future was up to me.

At home, Annie had moved out and was living with our sister Betty while working as an operator for Southern Bell. David married his long-term girlfriend and joined the Air Force. I missed them both.

That left Bill and me with our parents. Dad's declining health coupled with money problems were a bad combination. The retirement house on Long Holler Road was slowly coming along but was more primitive than what we had at Dry Gap Pike.

After a visit with Miss McGuire, the guidance counselor, I signed up for Distributive Education (DE), which allowed me to leave after a half day for a job coordinated by the school. I took the bus to Kresge's 5&10-cent store on Gay Street in Knoxville where I worked as a stock boy. Students got full credit toward graduation for DE.

During those trips downtown, the imposing University of Tennessee (UT) attracted my attention. Atop the hill on Cumberland Avenue, the brick edifices on the sprawling campus had a magnetism—in my imagination like the Empire State Building had in New York City. Traveling back 'n' forth on the bus, I let myself believe that college might be the road I could take. It was as if UT was calling out to me just as I was considering my next step.

Reflecting as I stared out the bus window about how I got to where I was—opportunity, a mouthful of a word for me—took on new meaning. My college dream started about the size of an acorn but the more I thought about it, the more the tiny acorn took root and started to sprout into a young oak. "College, gee-whiz—why not?" I asked myself as I got cranked at the concept.

With a fresh haircut and wearing a tucked-in, short-sleeved shirt, khaki pants, and newly shined shoes, I went to the UT campus on a day off. I was so excited as I walked onto the grounds that I tripped on an uneven section of sidewalk and nearly fell. Luckily, I recovered before anyone noticed.

I made my way to the agriculture department where the head instructor—a tall friendly-looking man with a broad smile—took the time to talk with me even though

I didn't have an appointment. I delivered a strong handshake and introduced myself, telling him about my experience doing farm work. Our talk raised my hopes. He showed me around while he explained the work-study program. He said there were positions open in the horticulture department with housing provided and that I would stand a good chance of being accepted.

On the way out, I felt better than I had in some time. But I still had zero money for college and neither did my parents.

I decided to talk to my brother Ray. The following day, I went to his office in downtown Knoxville to see if he could help me with tuition and the cost of books.

After confidently climbing the steps to his office in the old Journal Building on Gay Street, I told the secretary, an efficient-looking woman with cat-eye glasses adorned with rhinestones, that I was there to see my eldest brother. She pointed me toward his office.

Ray was sitting behind his desk and welcomed me.

"Hey Connie, what brings you here?" Ray stood up as I glanced around the office thinking it was smaller than I expected.

"Ray, you always told me it was important to get an education so I checked out the work-study program at UT," the words spilled out as I spoke faster than I'd intended. "I could get lodging in the horticultural building and my job would be looking after maintenance in the greenhouses. But I need help with tuition and any books."

Before Ray could speak, I blurted, "I was hoping you could find a way to help me and I thank you for what you have done for me in the past." I hadn't forgotten how Ray had kept my ass out of reform school.

Ray listened before answering and then looked right at me, saying he would tell me what he told our brother Don when he asked for financial assistance.

"Connie, you may remember when I came home from the war, I went to high school and college at the same time while working at the railroad."

There was a pause that seemed as long as the Tennessee River before Ray continued.

"It was very difficult," he said. "But if you prove to me you can get through the first two years, I'll see what I can do to help you. If you're really serious, you should be able to manage that."

Ray then went on to tell me the story about when he started his law practice. When he got his law degree, there were 2,000 lawyers in Tennessee and 500 were in

East Tennessee due to land-takings by the Tennessee Valley Authority (TVA), which was building a series of dams. The TVA project prevented flooding and created cheap electricity.

Ray pointed out that many of those lawyers went into practice with their fathers or grandfathers and didn't have to start out on their own. Pointing around the office with his right hand, he explained setting up a law practice was very expensive.

"This little 10-by-10 room that is 100 square feet is costing me $200 a month, not counting utilities and splitting the cost of our secretary with my law partner," he said. "The only thing I have to sell is my time and I charge by the hour."

I knew this was Ray's way of saying he couldn't afford to help me. He explained that Mom and Dad and other siblings had also asked him for help.

Staring at the brass lamp with a green glass shade on Ray's desk, I let my mind wander to the times when I was small and Ray would pinch my arm hard, nearly bringing me to tears. I hated him then. There were twenty years and fourteen siblings between us. I felt as though those pinches that left red marks were Ray's way of letting me know I was another mouth to feed in a family already stretched thin.

As I sat watching the lamp's brass pull chain move back 'n' forth due to a puff of wind from a cracked-open window, I didn't give Ray a verbal response. But he could surely tell from my frown and slumped shoulders how disappointed I was.

"Let's go across the street and get a cup of coffee," he said.

I followed him down the steps and across the street to the coffeeshop where we talked about other things. Feeling letdown, I couldn't recall anything we said over coffee that was of any consequence even a few minutes later.

As we left the coffeeshop and Ray headed back to his office, I was crestfallen and stared down at my feet as I shuffled along. A light rain had started to fall and the drops felt like tears running down my cheeks. I wasn't someone who cried—at least, I had no memory of crying in recent years as there was no point. The pitter-patter of the rain that picked up speed seemed to fill the emptiness I felt.

Two years of paying for college by myself with all the related costs seemed like an impossibility. My dream deflated instantly like a helium balloon poked by a sewing pin. I felt an overwhelming sense of sadness, realizing I had no one to turn to but myself. I was also angry as

I thought about the insurance money from my run-in with the panel truck and how some of that could be used for me to attend college. All I got from the settlement was an old junk car that I no longer owned. As I walked along, I repeated over and over to myself that I'd have to make other plans.

I remembered the main post office building across from the courthouse had the recruiting offices for the three branches of the service on the third floor and decided to check it out. Serving in the military had always been an option especially for boys from poor families like mine. After all, my six brothers had served. Military service was something a lot of my friends were considering.

The Army didn't require a high school diploma, but the Navy and Air Force did. Since I was somewhat knowledgeable about the Air Force through my brothers Bill and David, and would soon be a high school graduate, I decided I'd talk to them.

The recruiter, a sergeant wearing impressive dress blues, was welcoming. He asked if I had time to take the Air Force aptitude test right then and there, and I'd be contacted after graduation. I eagerly agreed to take the test that was divided into four categories: general, administration, mechanical, and electrical. As I left, I wasn't confident that I'd passed, but I felt better for having done it. It took my mind off my college disappointment.

∞∞∞∞∞∞∞∞∞∞∞∞∞∞∞∞∞∞∞∞∞∞∞∞∞∞

Once I turned eighteen the end of January, I counted the days until graduation. I was bored with school and to top it off, suddenly, the underclassmen seemed a lot younger.

Dad, Mom, and Bill were moving piecemeal to the house on the hillside on Long Holler Road but had to wait until warm weather because it didn't have any heat yet. Dad was fighting with the railroad to retire early due to his medical problems. While this was going on, I stayed at Dry Gap Pike, which was for sale but didn't have any takers right away.

Dad was sixty but looked older. He was a big man, heavy set, about six feet tall but seemed taller. His weathered face was like a roadmap. The lines all seemed to head downward. He no longer smiled or shared old stories. Apart from Bill and me, all his children had moved on with their lives. I stayed busy and kept out of his way.

Once Dad's retirement came through, my parents had to make do on Dad's pension and Bill's Air Force disability check—barely enough to live on. It was depressing. I contributed what I could from my odd jobs. Often Glen and Betty brought groceries over.

Before I knew it, my grade-school years were over. Graduation was in the auditorium at Halls Elementary School because there wasn't enough room for the Class of 1960 commencement at the high school. Mom, Betty, and Annie were in the audience to cheer me on.

But any pride I had on graduation day was cut short when I opened the case to my diploma only to find a sheet of paper inside that stated, "Due: one American history book."

At first, I was crushed and almost started crying. "This must be some mistake!" I thought. I knew I'd turned that book in.

Everyone kept asking to see my diploma and I didn't have it. Annie had a Brownie camera to get my picture and wanted me to open the cover. Making matters worse, I got the feeling that Mom and my sisters didn't believe me and thought I'd lost the book.

It was all I could do to keep from throwing the diploma case into the trash and taking off. I never wanted to see Halls High again.

I tossed and turned in bed all night.

Still roaring mad, I went to school the next day and confronted the history teacher. I told him I'd turned my book in the last day of class and put it on his desk.

I marched over to the bookshelf, found my book, and showed him my name in bold lettering in the back.

He made a lame effort to apologize but that didn't make me feel any better.

"Why didn't you let me know that I was missing a book and I could've straightened it out?"

He only shrugged and handed me a note to bring to the principal's office.

Note in hand, I strode to the office to pick up my diploma from the school secretary. I was still huffing and puffing. I held the note up, waving it above my head, and told her I'd been treated unfairly.

"You're not the only one that didn't get your diploma," she said as I stormed out, slamming the door behind me.

Once outside, I took a long, careful look at the diploma to make sure there were no spelling mistakes.

A few days later, I received a letter from the recruiter that I'd qualified for the Air Force. But I didn't give it another thought. I'd pretty much forgotten about enlisting.

<hr>

During my last month of school, I worked Saturdays at Cockrum Lumber Company in Knoxville doing odd jobs in the mill. After graduation, I started full-time, taking home thirty-five dollars a week. I couldn't afford a car and hitchhiked from Dry Gap Pike to Cockrum Lumber and back.

After about a week, I found a tiny efficiency apartment in the Broadway Apartments just a few blocks from Cockrum. Although we still saw each other occasionally, my relationship with Patsy was ending. She was heading into her sophomore year and wanted to hang out with the other students. I was no longer the handsome football player and popular guy but a working man with a regular job.

As the stress of having no money for a girlfriend got to me, I wasn't torn up when we drifted apart.

During my first week full-time, the shop manager assigned me to a workstation and told me to build myself a toolbox. I could borrow his tools for the time being but had to ask the secretary to order mine and pay for them through payroll deduction. I spent the better part of two days building the toolbox and painted it green.

At eighteen and a half, I was an adult and felt like I could see myself getting old.

Gone were my school days—and while they were never care-free—school was a lot more fun than what I found myself doing.

I had a small refrigerator in my apartment and mostly made boring bologna and cheese sandwiches for lunch. But one of my favorite places to eat was the Jiffy Burger where I could get a fifteen-cent hamburger.

One day at dinner, I sat at the counter facing a row of glass windows looking out onto the parking lot. A young man came in and sat down next to me. I noticed he'd left his headlights on.

"Hey, I think your lights are still on."

"Oh gosh! Thanks so much." He made a quick exit and came back in.

"Hey, my name is Elmer Nave." He extended his hand before sitting down. "That looks good."

He waved to the waitress and ordered the daily special: black coffee and chicken fried steak over mashed potatoes. His meal made my burger look pathetic.

"I'm Conley Ford. Is that a new car?"

"Yes, it's a brand-new Pontiac. I have a new car and a new job." Elmer was about five feet five inches and on the chubby side.

"Where do you work?"

"I just moved here from Kingsport. I have a job teaching shop at Christenberry Junior High."

"Jeez! I took shop at Christenberry before my family moved out of Knoxville."

Elmer, who was about four years older than me, graduated from Carson-Newman College. This was his first teaching job.

I mentioned I had a small efficiency apartment two blocks up the street for forty dollars a month.

"I have a big furnished apartment on the first floor of a house that I can't really afford. I've been looking for a roommate," Elmer said.

"I might be interested but have another couple of weeks paid up in my apartment."

Elmer drove me over to take a look. The apartment had a living room, one bedroom, kitchen, bathroom, and dining room that would serve as my bedroom. Since my part of the rent was less than I was paying for my apartment and Elmer's place was closer to work, I told him I could move in on the first of the month.

A week later, I met up with Elmer again at the Jiffy and said I was still interested. I started moving my things over to his place.

In the meantime, Cockrum Lumber thought I had potential and signed me up for a correspondence course with the Chicago Millworkers Architectural Institute on drafting and drawing. I made a drafting board out of a huge piece of plywood and bought a T-square to do the homework assignments in the apartment.

But as fall approached, I was making barely enough money to live on. Moving back home to cut expenses wasn't an option. Dry Gap Pike was sold. I didn't fancy piling in with Mom, Dad, and Bill in the primitive conditions at Long Holler Road.

At Cockrum, I was well liked and a good worker. But workdays had become monotonous. My coworkers were a lot older and supporting families. If anything could be said about my youth—it was unpredictable. I couldn't see myself adjusting to the tedious day-to-day routine at Cockrum.

While thumbing through my yearbook one night and reading messages from my classmates—I found the one from my buddy, Steve: *The best of everything to you Conley. I think you'll do good in life because you've got the guts to try.*

The Air Force letter I'd tucked into my yearbook, fell out. I looked it over and thought to myself, "Shit, I ain't going to get ahead doing what I'm doing. The service might be my way out."

The next day I gave my notice at Cockrum, picked up my toolbox, and took it to Betty's. Cockrum had been nice to me and we parted on good terms.

Elmer was dating the woman upstairs and they were talking about getting hitched. I suspected he was tired of my buddies from Halls showing up unannounced to hang out in the apartment and was relieved I planned to move on.

When I took off from home before, I didn't tell a soul and just left. In some ways my running-away adventures in New Orleans, Cincinnati, and Chicago seemed like they'd happened in a prior life. I knew I was no longer that thirteen-year-old hitchhiker bent on adventure and heading into the unknown. I was a young man considering my future.

Chapter Thirteen

AIR FORCE

A dozen recruits were milling around the Air Force office in downtown Knoxville when I arrived on the morning of Nov. 21, 1960. A sergeant asked us to line up and take a cursory physical. We stripped down to our skivvies.

I'd had school physicals in gym class that were more comprehensive. According to the doctor, my heart was beating fine, I could breathe well–despite being a smoker–and my muscles and bones were all okay. My backbone was nice and straight.

The sergeant said the physical fitness test after bootcamp would be tough and there were no guarantees the Air Force would keep us if we didn't pass with flying colors. I was unfazed. Being a high school athlete and working on a farm, I knew I was in good shape.

As we were filling out forms, one of the guys asked me about the question on religion.

"What's a religion, what does that mean?"

"That's where you go to church," I told him.

So, he wrote down "Sunny View Baptist Church." The sergeant just shook his head when he read it.

I took a deep breath as I turned in my questionnaire and got in the line to sign enlistment papers that would tie me up for four years. The guys ahead of me put their autographs down without delay. When it was my turn, I'll admit, I didn't read all the fine print. But it didn't matter, I'd made up my mind.

After all, my brothers Ray and Joe had served in the Navy; Henry and Don in the Army; and Bill and David in the Air Force. Our Dad hadn't served but he was proud of his older brother Tillman, who fought in France in World War I. Yup, the military seemed like the right way to go and I was cranked about heading out again on another adventure.

Using my best penmanship, I wrote my full name Conley Winston Ford in big letters.

The sergeant told us to be back there by 9 p.m.

I didn't get to say a proper goodbye to Elmer, who hadn't come home yet from his teaching job. I figured

I'd look him up when I came home on leave. I collected what little I had at the apartment and went to Betty's.

Betty had the night off from the telephone company. After I showered and cleaned up, we enjoyed some fried chicken with a good scald on it.

"Connie, you'll do well in the Air Force," Glen said. "They'll treat you right and you'll see the world."

I wondered if Glen had any regrets. I'd already been to a bunch of places. I guessed his age was about thirty-six. He'd grown up in Tennessee, married here, and stayed here.

Around 8:30 p.m., Betty insisted I call Mom and Dad and let them know my plans. Mom picked up, but Dad wasn't home. Although Mom was used to many goodbyes, she always got a little teary-eyed when one of her children was leaving. Mom told me to be careful and to write often.

After we hung up, I said my goodbyes to Betty, Glen, and the boys. I gave them a short salute before I sprinted down East Scott and jumped on the KTL bus back to the recruiting office. The bus went right through Happy Holler, which was just getting going for the night. While I didn't recognize anyone, the faces were eerily familiar.

Did they have dreams? How did they get stuck? I knew the answer. They stayed. I chose to leave.

I got to the recruiting office with five minutes to spare. Some of the other guys were already there. We lined up, raised our right hands, and took the Oath of Enlistment.

I glanced at my fellow recruits and thought the boys were around my age. For the most part, they were all scruffy looking, like they could use a haircut and a razor. I didn't have much to shave, as my beard was still coming in, but I'd made the effort to look my best. If this was my competition, I felt like I'd measure up.

Apart from a few nervous coughs, we were quiet on the military shuttle bus trip to the airport.

Walking on the tarmac to the plane, I got a good look at the shiny Lockheed Constellation and its four big propellers. Once on board, a sergeant told us the plane saw service transporting troops during World War II. It gave me a start when he said the Constellation was nicknamed "Connie."

<hr>

It got me to thinking about when I found out my name wasn't Connie but Conley.

My third-grade teacher Miss Cannon insisted on calling the roll, as written, on opening day. She was around thirty-five, tall, skinny, and stern. Behind her back, we called her an "old maid" because she hadn't married.

When no one answered to Conley, she informed me of my birth name, causing a room full of giggles.

She and I didn't get off to a good start. I guess I got into the habit of cutting up in class from that point on. This prompted Miss Cannon to write under the "conduct" section in my first report card: *Conley's conduct has been terrible*!

Dad was not pleased with this development. He scrawled in huge letters diagonally across the entire tri-folded report card where the message was clearly visible for the rest of the school year: *Miss Cannon, please take more off Conley's backside and less off his report card -- L. J. Ford.*

<hr/>

During the two-hour flight, I sat next to Lamonte, who'd graduated from the all-black Austin High School in Knoxville. We flew just above the low cloud cover, so we couldn't see much. Lamonte and I had the same goal: to get away. No one in his family had gone to college and he was the first to get a high school diploma. He was really proud of the Air Force, which he said was a cut above the other branches. Our chat helped me feel confident about my decision.

The flight made a refueling stop at Barksdale Air Base in northwest Louisiana where we picked up more recruits. We were allowed to get off the plane for half an hour, stretch our legs, and get a bite to eat.

While grabbing a burger, fries, and Coca-Cola at the mess hall, I made small talk with some of the other guys. One at my table was from Harlan, Kentucky and knew the area where my parents grew up. From what I could suss out, all of us were either from Kentucky, Tennessee, Louisiana, Mississippi, or Alabama.

During the ninety-minute flight to Lackland Air Force Base in San Antonio, I had time to think about my decision to enlist. I was no longer upset that my brother Ray didn't help me. Academics were not my strong suit and I knew it would've required a hell of an effort to succeed in college while holding down a job. I also couldn't see myself making a career at Cockrum Lumber.

As we approached San Antonio, the flat Texas landscape came into focus as the sun rose. I briefly wondered what might've happened if I'd headed to Brownsville that night when I left New Orleans. I inhaled deeply and exhaled. I was running off again but this time, I had a clear destination.

At Lackland, we joined other recruits and were assembled in groups of eighty, called a "flight." We had to march with our flight everywhere whether to the dining hall or over to get high-and-tight haircuts. In a huge green building, which we called the Green Monster, we got all our shots and were issued our clothing. They gave us a cardboard box to send our civilian clothes home.

New recruits were issued eight pairs of boxer shorts and t-shirts; one pair of shoes and two pairs of boots; and eight pairs of socks. Uniforms included a set of fatigues, field jacket, tans and dress blues, three hats, and two neckties.

It was more clothes than I'd ever had and what's more, they were all brand-new. I lifted the underwear to my nose to smell their newness.

Recruits were also issued two blankets, pillowcases, and sheets along with a footlocker. We were taught how to fold and roll, and neatly pack our clothes and how to mark everything with our serial number using a marking kit.

We were given a list of required necessities—gym clothes, a razor, shaving cream, soap, toothbrush, and toothpaste—and forty dollars for the PX (Post Exchange). The items totaled exactly $39.10. We spent the ninety cents in change during a break at the vending machines outside the barracks.

Our pay started at sixty dollars a month. I thought that was a good deal because it was all spending money. I wouldn't have to struggle like I did at Cockrum Lumber paying for food and my share of the rent and utilities.

At Lackland, I didn't have to pay for food, a place to sleep, my clothes, or laundry. Postage was even covered. I could deal with paying fifty cents for a haircut.

We were also issued three towels and wash cloths and showered every day, something I considered to be a real luxury. I used one of my towels to line the top tray in my footlocker where I laid out my toiletries. The Air Force required we shave every day whether we needed to or not.

We were shown how to make a bed so a quarter would bounce off of it.

With physical exercise, marching, going on the firing line, and other training—along with the daily task of shining our shoes and boots—we were busy all the time. I loved the reward structure in the military and knowing where I stood at all times.

After basic training, newly minted airmen take specialty courses depending on their aptitude and skills tests. I qualified to take the eight-week medical corpsman course which interested me. I learned medical terminology, how to change sheets with someone in bed, how to prep a patient for surgery, and how to sterilize instruments, among other tasks.

When I finished the course, my NCO (non-commissioned officer) called me in to talk about next steps.

"I see you're from Tennessee," he said.

"Yes, sir, that's right."

"I'm from Georgia. Are you a farm boy?"

"Yes, sir. You could say that." I told him about being in Future Farmers of America in high school. He knew all about the organization. He was also familiar with raising hogs, chickens, and stuff like that.

"A spot in veterinary tech school at Gunter AFB in Montgomery has opened up. It's a 10-week course. Interested?" The course also included food inspection of dairy and meat products.

I liked the sound of it and was happy to be asked. I didn't hesitate to say, "Yes, sir!" Within a few days I got my orders and was on my way to Alabama.

<hr>

After the course, I was stationed at Sewart Air Force Base in Smyrna, Tennessee where I was a veterinary tech assisting the doctors in the animal clinic. I also worked as a food inspector on base.

When on leave, I would hitchhike the four hours to Knoxville every two or three months. When I wore my uniform, it was easy to get a ride.

At home I'd visit Mom and Dad. With limited indoor plumbing and no central heat, their tiny, two-bedroom house on Long Holler Road was barely habitable.

There were no airs about my parents at all, no snobbery of any kind—they adjusted to their conditions as if they'd never left them. They were spending their older years living in the same poverty they'd grown up with. The neighbors on Long Holler Road were even poorer than they were.

On these trips, I stayed with Betty on East Scott Avenue and thumbed around.

During one visit after I helped castrate a boar, Dad gave me a letter he'd penned to my superior officers at Sewart. Dad was amused that I'd become a veterinary tech—training, he believed–was a waste of time because I'd dealt with animals all my life.

In the note, he said while I was getting ready to castrate a couple of pigs, I mistook a sow for a male. The angry sow then bit me on the seat of my pants, tearing a hole big enough to throw a dog through. Dad wrote:

Connie was more nervous than a long-tailed cat in a room full of rocking chairs and took off.

That was the only part of the note that could be shared in polite company. The rest was peppered with foul language as he described how I'd botched a couple of the castrations.

It was all made up, but I didn't get the humor. I never delivered the letter and Dad never asked me about it. But years later, I was glad I'd kept it. It was written in Dad's longhand with an indelible pencil.

Dad had no idea what I'd experienced at Sewart and I didn't care to tell him. Sympathy was not one of my Dad's glowing traits. I never talked to him about things that bothered me because I didn't think he'd care to listen.

In October during the Cuban Missile Crisis, I'd been part of Operation Gray Eagle and sent to help reopen a boarded-up World War II-era field hospital at Opa-loca Air Naval Station in Florida. Our mission was to clear the facility of mold and rodents so it could receive casualties from the potential invasion of Cuba. It was a grueling, dirty job.

Using huge pieces of plywood on sawhorses, we set up field kitchens. We thought we were going to war and within twenty-four hours, some 10,000 soldiers and marines arrived by train. The lines at our makeshift kitchen were blocks long. I could sense the nervous energy in the air during the ramp-up. It was my first-time being part of a real mission where everybody had a common purpose. I could feel the electrifying energy that bolted through the air like lightning.

But what has forever stayed with me, were two Air Force plane crashes at Sewart just three months apart.

The Sewart base hospital was short-staffed. Because of my medical corpsman training, I was called in to assist with the autopsies of the airmen.

While I was used to death in animals—this was way beyond my experience.

The pilot in the first accident ejected upside down right into the runway, turning his head to jelly. He was shuttling a T-33, two-seater jet trainer, across the country. He was taking off in the morning to continue flying to Hunter Air Force Base in Georgia when he couldn't get enough altitude because the engine flamed out.

The second incident involved a C-130 Hercules that lost two engines during a training flight and crashed. The five crewmembers, stuck in a hunched-over position, were burnt beyond recognition. They weren't much older than me.

I had to help retrieve the bodies and place them in body bags. The airmen were all tangled up in insulation and wiring that had melted in the heat. The soles of their boots were still on their feet but the tops had burned off. We brought them to the morgue where we had to take the contorted bodies out of the body bags for x-rays. The sight and stench were overwhelming. The pathologist gave us Vicks Vaporub to put under our noses to camouflage the smell. The air force photographer couldn't handle it and left.

The memories of those horrific events come back without warning. I might be driving, showering, or sitting at my desk, when the unsettling scenes come out of nowhere and replay in my mind.

Dealing with the aftermath of those plane crashes was a hell of a way to grow up. Any remnants of the boy inside me was gone. Nightmares kept me from sleeping right for weeks. But I sucked it up and didn't complain. It was years before I'd talk to anyone about it.

<hr />

When I'd been in the service about eighteen months, I was promoted to Airman First Class. I got ready for deployment to Wheelus Air Base in Tripoli in the Kingdom of Libya to work with the veterinarians. I'd never heard of Wheelus and knew nothing about Libya.

My only experience outside the country was a couple of quick trips on a weekend pass at Lackland across the border to Boy's Town in Nuevo Laredo. My buddies and I would hit the topless dance clubs and local bars where the beer was cheap.

I checked out a map and saw that Libya was in northern Africa and was right next to Egypt. We'd learned about the pyramids in school.

———

Taking a few days of leave before deployment, I headed to Knoxville. I connected with some of my friends and stopped by to see Elmer, who was engaged to the woman upstairs. He seemed really happy.

I spent a half day out at Long Holler helping Dad and Bill with some repairs. Dad liked to build things and showed me an adult-sized cradle he'd made. He used some plywood to make the bottom and sides and put oak rockers on the bottom. Inside was an old, skinny mattress that'd come from a cot.

Dad said rocking back 'n' forth was a good way to get exercise and get to sleep. He thought it might be marketable. I nodded my support but declined to try it out because it was kind of creepy.

Before I left to go back to Betty's and return to Sewart, Dad said he wanted to have a word with me.

"Connie, you won't see me alive again," he said. He was so curt and matter of fact that I couldn't take him seriously.

"Come on, Dad. Don't say that."

He looked away and went back to sanding his invention.

I shrugged Dad's comment off. He was such a powerful force in my life that I couldn't fathom him giving into anything.

I left without telling Dad I loved him.

<hr/>

Getting to Wheelus was a major journey. I took a bus to Charleston Air Force base where I flew to Bermuda, to Santa Maria in the Azores, to Casablanca, and finally to Wheelus.

Wheelus comprised twenty square miles on the Mediterranean. The sea was like a huge lake, not choppy at all. The beaches were beautiful, almost as nice as those in Florida.

The palm trees produced big bundles of dates not coconuts. I could eat them like candy. Using a machete with a large hooked tip, Libyan men shinnied up the date palms to harvest the fruit.

Texas was hot and Tennessee could be an oven in the summer, but nothing like Libya. It was upwards of 100 degrees and we often got sandstorms called Ghibli that blew off the Sahara Desert. The sand was a fine powder and stuck to the moist areas around our mouths, noses, and eyes. It coated everything in our quarters. We put wet towels under the doors and windows to try to keep the stuff out.

After a few months at Wheelus, I'd been drinking a few cans of Tennents beer with a Libyan civilian friend, Nuri. He was dating an American secretary at the base. We were standing on the patio at his villa.

I reached for another beer and cut my thumb badly on the pull-tab.

"Yow! That hurt." I went to the bathroom and used my handkerchief to wrap my thumb tightly to stop the bleeding. When I came back out, I told Nuri I had to leave because I needed stitches. Nuri spoke with an English accent and sounded like the film star David Niven.

"Conley, when you are having fun and unexpectedly injure yourself badly—that's a sign that something has happened in your family."

I went to the emergency room at the base hospital where the airman on duty had to wake up the doctor, who was not happy about being roused for stitches. It didn't help matters that I'd had quite a few beers and was slurring my speech.

Back at my quarters, I threw away my bloody handkerchief and hit the sack. About two hours later, I jumped up when there was a loud, rapid knock at the door.

The Charge of Quarters told me to go to the Red Cross Office. I jumped into my pants and shirt and rushed over to the Red Cross. I thought something had happened to Mom or Bill.

The clock at the Red Cross office said 3 a.m. The advisor told me to sit down and that he had sorrowful news. He said my father had died of heart failure. I had to sit down to collect myself. Dad was sixty-two years old.

I returned to my quarters and couldn't sleep as thoughts raced through my mind. I was unable to accept the news. That morning, I arose early, packed a small duffel bag, and was cut orders to fly home on emergency leave.

Once on the plane, all the years of never having cried suddenly flooded up inside me and I bawled. My shoulders heaved with each sob. Once the tears came, they were unstoppable. I was inconsolable, so much so that the stewardess on the military flight was worried about me. She kept checking on me, asking if there was anything she could do. The airman beside me must have been uncomfortable but showed respect by being quiet.

How could I be so heartbroken? I wasn't sure I understood why. Family and friends had said I was more like my Dad than any of my siblings. Dad and I shared a few good moments together when I came home on leave from Sewart. I think he realized I was no longer a boy and treated me like a man, almost an equal.

The tears continued to fall as I recalled the day Dad took me shopping for a car after my '49 Ford bit the dust. We went and looked at cars but I knew he didn't have any money.

I sobbed so much on the flights home that I hurt physically and mentally. I cried for my loss and the loss of not doing more for my Dad. I knew he was having a tough time. None of us had shown Dad any sympathy with his being eaten up by psoriasis and stomach problems. He'd struggled to make ends meet and his stress level was always in the stratosphere.

How could a man like my Dad be gone? His deep voice was as powerful as his distinctive personality. When he spoke loudly, he could be heard a block away. He could be scary while at the same time, his tall tales about his youth and early marriage years had listeners in stitches.

The flights back home took forever. I had to take a Greyhound Bus from Charleston to Knoxville. The entire journey from Wheelus to home took about twenty-four hours.

I got out at Magnolia Avenue and walked from there to Betty's where Glen heated up some biscuits.

I was a mess at the funeral that drew a big crowd including my parents' neighbors, the Wrights—who were as poor as a church mouse. I was shocked to see Uncle Tillman, my dad's only living brother, was the spitting image of Dad. My former girlfriend Patsy came with her parents to the burial service. It meant a lot to me. She was dating someone new and I'd moved on with my life. But her presence showed we'd always mean something to each other.

After the funeral, I pulled myself together but I still felt fragile inside—a feeling that I'd never had before. I made sure to tell Mom I loved her and hugged her before returning to Wheelus.

Back at Wheelus, I kept my grief bottled up during the day when performing my duties. But at night, before finally getting to sleep, I wept inside my mind, not outwardly. I wept for knowing I couldn't take anything back; that Dad was gone forever. Now it seemed to me that Dad was misunderstood by me and my siblings.

Dad told us if something needed to be done, then do it without being asked. If a neighbor's yard was overgrown, then cut it. If he saw the neighbor's kids without shoes, the next time we got shoes—he gave them ours. If we had food on our table and someone he knew did not, then he gave some of ours away.

We hated that at the time. We worked hard and couldn't understand Dad's generosity at our expense. But that was the way he was. He had no patience for whining or laziness.

I came to realize Dad was a man of his times: hard times, Depression times. Through all the disappointment, struggles and heartache, he and Mom had sixteen children—fourteen of whom lived to adulthood. All of us knew the value of hard work and how to survive.

Maybe that was his legacy. We learned to take care of ourselves.

EPILOGUE

Conley Ford at thirteen.

By Conley Ford

By sharing my story, I am not advocating for any boy or girl to follow my path by taking off and trying to make it on their own. The world is a far more dangerous place than it was in 1955 when I was just thirteen years old.

I hope my experiences demonstrate it's possible to come through a hardscrabble childhood and succeed in life.

Enlisting in the Air Force was one of the best decisions I ever made. The Air Force provided me with a wealth of opportunity that included education, promotion, and travel. The GI Bill helped me buy my first house.

I figured if I could get promoted in the Air Force, then I could do the same in the private sector. I found the biggest company I could. I retired thirty-five years later after a rewarding career with Western Electric and Bell Communications Research.

By taking classes on nights and weekends, I realized my dream of going to college. I graduated with honors from Wentworth Institute of Technology in Boston, Massachusetts.

At this writing, I have been married for forty-eight years to a former teacher and journalist who wrote *Boy at the Crossroads*, inspired by my youth.

Like many of you, I had a difficult dad.

My deepest hope is that my two sons, Jarat and James—of whom I am immensely proud—will read *Boy at the Crossroads* and come away with a better understanding of what made me the father I was.